WITCH CURSED IN WESTERHAM

Paranormal Investigation Bureau Book 10

DIONNE LISTER

For Ben.

CHAPTER 1

"Mmm, it smells so good in here." Saliva drenched my mouth and spurted out before I could close my lips.

Imani, waiting with me in Tulsi's Indian restaurant for our takeaway, screwed up her face. She frantically wiped her cheek. "Gross, Lily. You even contaminated my lips. Your salivary glands are out of control. Calm them, please."

I pressed my lips together, then held my palm over my mouth as I spoke… just in case some rogue drops shot out. "I'm so sorry. I didn't mean it. You don't have to worry, though. I don't have any diseases or anything." She looked at me, one eyebrow elevated. "Well, it's not like I can take it back. Do they have a bathroom here? Maybe you could go wash your face?"

An Indian lady dressed in a vibrant green sari

approached us with two plastic bags. Phew, saved. "Here's your order, loves. Enjoy your meal." She smiled.

I grinned in return and took the bags. "Thank you. This smells delicious." Imani gave me a side-eyed glance. We turned and left.

Once out on the footpath, a burst of high-energy, almost hyperactive magic slapped the back of my skull before dissipating. That was weird. I looked at Imani. "Did you feel that?"

Her gaze flicked up and down the street. "Yes." There was nothing obvious out of place.

"It was strong. Should we be worried?" My heart beat faster because even though I didn't have the feeling of being watched, it was possible that RP—Regula Pythonissam, the group who were after me—were out there, observing. I threw up a return-to-sender spell just in case.

"I don't know, Lily. Whatever it was, it's gone now." Imani's phone rang. "Hello, James. Yes." Imani looked across and down the street a bit. "Okay. Yep. Bye." She turned to me. "I have to attend a potential crime scene, which happens to be that antique shop over there." She pointed to where she'd been looking a moment ago—at a two-storey white semi-detached building with the sign Castle Antiques Centre mounted on the building above the glass shopfront. Like many English buildings, a dormer window at the top of the building indicated there was liveable space in the roof cavity.

"I love antique shops. Lead the way. Actually, what sort

of crime? We're not about to walk into a shop full of blood and guts, are we?" Because that wouldn't be fun, obviously.

"Stolen items that just popped out. The owner's a witch, so she called the PIB straight away." Imani looked both ways and crossed. I stayed on her heels. The owner met us at the front door.

The thirty-something-year-old had brown hair in two braids, one over each shoulder. She was a fellow nail-biter, a finger currently in her mouth. She didn't even bother taking the finger from her lips when she spoke. She eyed us. "Are you from the PIB?"

"Yes. I'm Agent Jawara, and this is my assistant, Lily Bianchi." Imani wasn't in uniform today, as she technically didn't start her shift until three, but she pulled out her ID and showed the woman.

The shop owner held out her hand—the one that had been partly in her mouth—for Imani to shake. Imani looked at it, paused, then quickly shook it. Ew. I gave the woman a quick nod and folded my arms. I didn't want to give her the impression I wanted to shake her manky hand.

"Thanks for coming so quickly. I'm Lissa."

"Why don't you take us inside and explain what happened? I'll need to get an inventory of what was taken, and if you have any photos of the missing items, that would be helpful."

"Of course." She turned and led us inside.

The stale smell of old furniture and the fresh scent of eucalyptus oil seeped from the pores of the quiet interior. It was mildly pleasant, and, for a moment, I could've been in the past.

We reached a wider spot in the narrow path threading through tightly packed furniture and shelves holding plates, teacups, vases, and all manner of collectable knick-knacks. Lissa halted and pointed to either side of the aisle. "This side had a pair of 19th Century Doulton of Lambeth Plinths." She turned. "This side had a round Regency mahogany four-seat dining table. All up, they're worth around five-thousand pounds, give or take." She frowned.

Imani made notes in a small notepad. "When did you notice they were missing, and how did you discover it?"

"It was about five or six minutes ago. I was sitting behind the counter"—she nodded at the counter at the back of the shop—"looking towards the door, and I felt a bit of magic; then they just popped away. I don't even know how that's possible. No one was here to cast a spell on them."

Imani pulled out her phone and took photos of the spaces. She mumbled something, and her magic grazed my scalp. Imani smiled. "We have a signature." She said, "Symbol, you've made an impression on me. I'm taking your image and sending it to the PIB." She looked at Lissa. "Someone would have had to come in here at some point and cast the spell that would eventually have taken the furniture away. Do you have security cameras?"

"No. We don't normally have a problem with theft, and I have mirrors everywhere, so I can always keep an eye out."

I looked around. Rounded convex mirrors were positioned near the ceiling in each of the four corners, so she would have had a good view from wherever in the shop she happened to be. Imani's gaze landed on my face. She raised an eyebrow. Did she want me to take photos? But we couldn't risk anyone finding out what it was I did. I gave a quick head shake. Imani turned back to the woman. "I think we need more formal photos. I'm going to get my assistant to take them. Do you mind?"

She shrugged. "If you think it will help. Okay."

"You can wait at your counter if you like. We won't be long."

"Fine." She made her way behind said counter and sat on a stool but continued to observe us.

Since she was a witch, it was fine for me to magic my Nikon to myself. I placed the two bags of food on the floor, took the lens cap off, turned the camera on, and pointed it at the aisle next to where the furniture used to be. I didn't want to say anything out loud, in case Lissa heard me. *Show me who stole the furniture that disappeared today.*

The lighting changed slightly, and I turned towards the window. It was raining on the day the items were spelled. I turned to face the back of the shop where Lissa sat. A man stood between me and her, blocking my view of the counter. He was side-on to me, touching one of the plinths. Unfortunately, he wore a baseball cap pulled low over his face, sunglasses, and a thick brown beard covered the rest of his face. His long coat hid his build. The only meaningful information I could get was his height—about five ten—his hair, and white skin.

I wanted to get a shot of Lissa on that day so we could

pinpoint which day the man had come into the shop. At the risk of losing the moment in my lens, I flicked my gaze back and forth from the camera to my surroundings as I moved through the shop—I was liable to knock something over since it was so cluttered.

I rounded the corner into the next aisle. There she was, in grey woollen slacks, a sky-blue jumper, and grey beanie. It must have been cold that day, which makes sense since it was winter. Lissa had been talking to an old lady, who held up a pretty plate decorated with colourful birds. I took a few shots and came around to the aisle with the thief from the other direction. Bummer. I frowned. This angle didn't give me any more insight into what he looked like, but I snapped away, just in case something revealed itself later when we zoomed in on the picture.

I turned my camera off. "Agent Jawara, I'm done."

"Thanks, Bianchi." She couldn't call me agent, so that was better than Assistant Bianchi. I smiled. To be honest, I kind of liked the sound of it. The blokeyness was cool. Imani walked over to Lissa. "Do you have photos of the items?"

"Here," she said and turned her laptop around so Imani could see the screen. Even though I had photos of the items from the past, it would be weird if she didn't ask for them. We didn't want to give any inkling of what my talent was.

Imani took photos of the screen with her phone. When she finished, she slipped her phone in her pocket and pulled out her notebook and pen again. "Have you had any customers use magic in your store in the last few weeks?"

Lissa turned the laptop back around and drummed her fingers on the marble countertop. "I don't usually pay much attention, except to make sure no one's stealing anything. In the last couple of weeks, I'd say maybe three people? I can't be sure, though."

Imani jotted down the information. "Can you give me a description of those people?"

"Um… there was a young couple in here, guy and girl, and they both used magic, but it was only because he forgot his wallet, and she magicked home the chair they bought after they paid for it. There was a man in here about a week ago." Her eyes opened wide. "Come to think of it, he was checking out the table. Not sure about the plinths , but I definitely saw him touch the table. After that, I had to help another shopper, and, actually, that's when he used magic. It wasn't a lot though, and I briefly checked in the mirrors to make sure he hadn't taken anything. By the time I came around to see if he wanted help, he'd gone."

"And what did he look like?"

"He had on a dark cap, sunglasses, and a dark jumper, or maybe a coat. He had a normal build—oh, and a beard. I can't remember any other specifics. To be truthful, I wasn't paying that much attention as I was serving someone else. So many people come in and out, I could never recall exactly what people were wearing. I'd be terrible picking out of a line-up." She brought her hand to her mouth and chewed a fingernail.

"Don't worry about it. You'd be surprised at how much people get wrong in these situations. We'll let you know if we find anything in our database that matches the magic signature. In the meantime, if anything else happens, or something comes to mind, let me know. Here's my card." Imani handed her a white, rectangular square.

"Thank you. And if that man returns, I'll definitely let you know straight away."

A gentle smile lit Imani's face. "Great. Do you mind if we travel from here?" We'd walked to the shop from Angelica's, but now there was an investigation, it was likely we'd have to go straight to the PIB with the evidence.

"Not a problem. You can go back there." She pointed to a doorway on the back wall, just to the right of her counter.

Imani picked up both bags of food. "Thanks."

I followed her into the storage room and shut the door. Imani made her doorway. Turning to me, she said, "PIB."

I nodded. After she left, I made my doorway and did the same.

◈

When we arrived at the PIB, Gus answered the reception-room door. After informing us that Ma'am was out, he led us down the hallway, recounting the latest dog-vomiting incident. "The missus walked out and left me to clean it up. Can you believe that?" He laughed and shook his head. Oh, I could believe it all right.

"Maybe you missed your calling, Gus."

"How's that, Agent Jawara?" he asked.

"You should've gotten into nursing or childcare, since

you don't mind cleaning up vomit, and you'd have even more stories." Imani glanced at me and smirked. *Gah, don't encourage him!* I narrowed my eyes, warning her to stop.

Even though the timing was off, my stomach grumbled. The plastic bag filled with Indian yumminess swung from Imani's hand. "Um, excuse me."

Imani looked back at me. "Yes?"

"Since Ma'am isn't here, can we go sit in the cafeteria and eat?"

Imani shrugged. "I suppose it wouldn't hurt. Okay, then." She looked at Gus. "Lovely seeing you. I hope your dog feels better soon."

He smiled and waved his hand dismissively. "He'll be fine. He vomits all the time. It's just him."

I waved. "Bye, Gus. See you later."

"Bye, Miss Lily. Have a lovely day."

"You too." I smiled as he stopped and turned to head back the other way. Imani and I went towards the lift. "I might see if Liv wants to join us."

"Great." We reached the lift, and she pressed the button. Her phone rang. "Agent Jawara speaking." She made some noncommittal noises and listened. "Yes, Ma'am. Okay. Be there in a moment. Bye." She frowned and handed me the bag of food. "I'm sorry, Lily, but I've been called out on another job. Don't worry about saving me any. I'll just grab something from the cafeteria when I get back."

"Are you sure? Weren't you looking forward to it?" I didn't know if I could just give up my Indian food like that if I'd been so close to eating it. I probably would've told

Ma'am I'd be ten minutes, and that's why I couldn't be an agent—priorities.

"I can get more later. You enjoy it with Liv. I'll speak to you later about getting those photos. Bye, love."

"Bye." I waved as she disappeared through her doorway. Alone in the corridor, my shoulders slumped. I'd been looking forward to having lunch with Imani. Had I mentioned lately how much I hated surprises?

I magicked my camera home, then slid my phone out of my pocket to call Liv. The phone rang and rang and rang. She finally picked up just before it went to voicemail. "Hey, Lily." She sounded frazzled.

"Hey. I'm heading to the cafeteria with some Indian food. Interested in joining me? Imani and I were meant to have lunch, but she's been called away on an urgent job."

"Um, I'd love to, but I'm flat out. Do you want to come up and eat in my office? I can eat and work."

"Yeah, sure. See you in a minute." I hung up and made my way through empty hallways to her and Millicent's office. Millicent was having a few months off on maternity leave, so Liv had the space all to herself in the meantime. When I reached her door, I didn't bother knocking before opening it. "Hey, it's me!" I shut the door and continued through the reception area to the office.

Liv was in front of her computer with files piled up to one side on her desk. Every few seconds, her computer dinged, as if she were getting a message. She looked at me and smiled a somewhat stressed smile. "Hey. That smells good. Thanks for coming up. Sorry I couldn't meet you downstairs. Today's been crazy." She blew out a full breath, lifting a curl that had settled in front of one eye.

I put the food on Millicent's desk, took my coat off, and hung it on one of her guest chairs, then sat. "I noticed it was quiet out there. What's going on?"

"About two hours ago, the phones went nuts. We've had thirty call-outs to witch-related crimes throughout Hampshire, Kent, Somerset, and Surrey. Mainly thefts. It's crazy. There's hardly anyone left at headquarters, and the calls keep coming. I'm liaison." Her computer dinged again, and she stuck her bottom lip out in a sad pout. "The messages just don't stop. Hang on a sec." She turned back to her computer and started typing.

Thankfully, over the last three weeks, Beren and Doctor Finnegan had tested the magic in my stupid snake tattoo. They hadn't turned the tracking off yet, which was frustrating to say the least because Regula Pythonissam knew where I was at all times, but Beren had ascertained I wasn't a danger to Liv. If I had been, there was no way I'd be allowed to be alone with her. I had missed hanging out, just the two of us.

To make things easier for Liv, I set the food out, magicked two sets of cutlery and two plates onto the table, and filled one plate for her. I set it on the side of her desk that didn't have all the files. "Here you go. Is there anything I can help you with?"

She stopped typing and turned to me. "This is fabulous, thanks. Food is all I need right now, and it's nice to have company."

I sat back down in the guest chair in front of Mill's desk, and we ate in silence for a few minutes. Mmm, this food was delicious. I hadn't had food from there before, but I'd be going back for sure.

Just as I was about to shovel another forkful of curry into my mouth, a piercing alarm sounded. Stunned, my arm jerked, flinging my food across the room to splat against the wall before falling to the floor. I dropped my fork and slammed my hands over my ears.

Liv swivelled around to stare at me, her eyes wide, her hands also protecting her ears. The horrific noise continued, and she jumped up, jerking her head towards the door, ears still covered. This must be a drill or something, but, man, was it loud. Time to follow Liv and get outside.

I silently bade goodbye to the food on my plate. *I'll be back for you later. Stay safe, my spicy friends.*

Out in the corridor, I would've expected people to be running everywhere, but there was just Liv, me, and one other middle-aged woman. I looked at her with my other sight, confirming she was a non-witch, so she must be someone's secretary. Her high-heeled black shoes clicked a fast beat as we headed to the lift. When we got there, I read the sign: In case of fire, do not use lift. So, did that mean no one was ever allowed to use the lift, in case there happened to be a fire? I snorted to myself. Obviously, they meant in a case where there *is* a fire, but their wording was stupid.

"Well, we'll have to take the stairs," said Liv. "I don't think there's a fire, but we should probably be careful. The exit's this way. I should've just gone straight there. Come on." The lady followed us as we hurried along the passage-way. We went through the emergency exit into the stairwell and descended, finally exiting into the freezing air and park-like grounds.

Stupid me had left my coat on the chair. Liv stopped a few metres from the building and hugged herself. "It's a bit chilly."

I laughed. "Trust you to understate how cold it is. Typical Brit. Lucky you have me. Where was your coat?"

"On the hook behind the door."

"Thanks." I held out both hands. "Within Millicent's office are two coats: one on a chair, and one hanging from the door. Please send them to me now, I implore." Magic trickled out of me, and the jackets appeared, one hanging on each arm. I handed Liv hers and donned mine.

"You *are* very handy to have around, Lily. Thank you."

I smiled. "It's my pleasure." I bowed as if she were royalty, and she giggled. I straightened. Two men exited where we had and walked past to stand with the woman who'd come out just after us. All in all, there were maybe twelve people standing around. The alarm was still blaring, but it wasn't as loud out here. I grabbed Liv's arm and took her further from the building, where it was quieter. "What do you think is happening?"

She shrugged. "I thought maybe it was a drill, but the alarm should've stopped by now."

Powerful magic skittered along my scalp and down my spine. I gasped. As uncomfortable as it was, it didn't have a distinct feel about it, or, rather, it had too much within it to pick out anything clearly. Was it more than one witch performing the same spell?

"Are you okay, Lily?" Liv touched my arm.

"Ah, someone's drawing magic. A lot of magic." Normally, I'd feel the odd ping of magic at the PIB, but generally nothing much, just enough to make photocopies, or move food around the place etcetera. "I think you should call Ma'am." I would've run in to see what was going on, but I had no idea where to start—it was a ginormous building.

She wrinkled her forehead. "Okay. Should I ask her to return?"

"Definitely."

While she called Ma'am, Gus appeared at the same door we'd come from, holding his head and stumbling. "Gus!" I shouted and ran towards him. The waves of magic grew stronger and the alarm peals louder the closer to the building I got. I didn't fancy shouting at him, so I grabbed his arm to help him away, but dizziness struck me. I kept hold of him and slammed my other hand against the wall for balance. This was crazy. What the hell was going on?

I mashed my lips and teeth together against the need to retch. The longer I stood there, the worse the dizziness became, until I was ready to fall. We had to get away.

I sucked in a deep breath. This was it. We just had to go, whether we were on our feet or not. I pushed off the wall and lurched forward, dragging Gus along. Every step lessened the wooziness. When we reached Liv, only the dregs of nausea remained, although the alarm still screeched. A headache needled behind my eyes. I released Gus, put my hands on my knees, and took some deep breaths.

Gus rubbed the back of his head. "I have to go back in there."

I straightened. "That's impossible. I can't believe you managed to make it outside. I would've been lying on the floor in my own vomit if I'd stood there much longer."

Gus cringed. "No offence, Miss Lily, but that's disgusting. I already feel sick. There's no need to add to it."

My mouth dropped open. So dog vomit was okay, but human vomit was off limits? I'd have to remember not to be so polite next time he regaled me with his *delightful* stories. I turned to Liv. "Did Ma'am say she was coming? Because she should probably avoid the reception room." Could whatever spell was there kill people?

"She said she was on her way. What happened over there, anyway? You two don't look too well."

"There's some kind of magic. If you get too close, you get really dizzy and want to"—I eyeballed Gus—"expel the contents of your stomach." He nodded. At least that description must have been okay, which was silly, since we all knew what I meant. "We have to warn her. Maybe she can travel away quickly. Can you call her again?"

"I'll try."

"While you do that, I'll contact Will." I'd hate for him to get called back for the emergency and then he succumbed too. Thank goodness he picked up straight way. "Hey, Will, sorry to bother you, but there's a… situation at the PIB."

"Is that an alarm I can hear in the background?"

"Yes. But don't travel to the reception room whenever you come back—there's some sick-making kind of spell. I'm not sure what's happened, but it's too strong for me to even go into the building. Gus is out here with Liv and me. He isn't too well." Gus's face still had a distinct green tinge.

"Does Ma'am know?"

"Yes, well, not the whole thing. Liv told her to hurry and come back, but she didn't tell her about the spell. She's trying her again now." Two PIB agents—a man and a woman—crawled out of the door. They made it a few feet, then collapsed. Crap. "Um, Will, two agents just crawled out of the door. They don't look good at all. I think they're unconscious."

Will swore. "Lily, I'm going to have to come. I'll bring B. But I need you to do something."

"Whatever it is, I'm there."

"You're going to have to make a landing spot for us, then send us the coordinates."

I swallowed. I'd never done anything as complex before. I knew stuffing up the landing spot could send an agent anywhere, even the middle of the ocean or the centre lane of a busy road. There was no room for error. I took a deep breath. "Okay. Tell me what I have to do." Liv was still trying to get hold of Ma'am, so I told Gus what I was doing and walked further from the building, to a spot on the grass away from everyone.

"Okay. I've found a level spot out the front of the building." Butterflies added to the aftermath of nausea in my stomach—not my favourite feeling in the world.

"You're going to step out a circle big enough for two people to occupy. As you do that, I'm going to get you to use your magic to draw a golden line. At the end of it, it should look like a hoop on the ground. Does that make sense?"

"Yes." This, I could handle. I crossed my fingers that it didn't get much more complicated.

"And make sure the line doesn't fade. It needs to stay there until we banish it. Okay?"

"Okay." I swallowed, my nerves deciding maybe it wasn't going to be that straightforward after all.

"Oh, and it has to be strong enough to hold the spell you're going to place inside."

"Right. Any other requests? Would you like the colour to pulse as well, maybe add in some blue and red flashes? Because the more stuff you want me to do, the less likely it is that I'm going to be able to make it work." Channelling that woman at the antique shop from this morning, I bit my fingernail. At least Imani wasn't here to rib me about it, but actually, if she had been here, she'd do this spell, not me.

"Don't worry, Lily. This isn't the hard part. You'll do fine. You're the one with multiple special talents, remember? If anyone can do this, it's you. I wouldn't ask you to do something I didn't think you could handle. Okay?"

I took a shuddering breath. "Mmmhmm. If you say so. Right. I'll let you know when it's done." I kept him on the line.

The stronger you wanted the spell, the more power you had to put into it. I opened the portal to the golden river, my stomach warming as the energy entered my body. I imagined the energy coming out of my feet and said, "Make a golden circle on the ground, following my steps as I walk around. Make the circle strong enough to contain a powerful spell, and don't let it disappear until I tell you to." I started walking, carefully placing one foot in front of the other, creating a neat circle. Brilliant golden light burst forth from beneath my shoes as I went. When I closed the circle, I stepped back and admired the shining round beacon hovering just above the stunted winter grass.

I raised the phone to my ear. "Done. Now what?"

"It isn't fading?"

"Nope. It's bright, no fading spots. I thought you said I'd be able to do it easily. Now the truth comes out." I couldn't blame him, really, considering I'd never done it before, but this didn't bode well for his confidence in me to do the next part right.

"Sorry. I do trust you. Ignore me being silly. Are you ready for the next part? Once you make this spell, we'll be able to land there."

"Yep, I'm ready." The alarm continued blaring in the background. I glanced at Liv and Gus, who were talking, worried expressions on their faces. Liv was gesticulating at the building. She likely hadn't been able to contact Ma'am. Crap. I had to shove that out of my thoughts so I didn't make things worse by sending Will and Beren to the moon.

"In order for you to know the coordinates, you'll need to stand inside the circle and tap into the magical world map. Once you know the coordinates, you'll use them in the spell."

Ma'am had shown me once before how to tap into the world map and focus in on a point. You could only get coordinates if you were standing in the spot. There was a book of coordinates, which gave all the public-toilet landing spots in the world, but you could only get coordinates for a person's reception room, for instance, if they gave it to you, or if you stood in it and looked it up that way. At least it made things more secure.

I stepped back into the shining hula hoop. Closing my eyes, I pictured the world as a globe in space. It spun slowly until I saw the UK. I focussed on it, drawing it toward me. "Show me the coordinates for where I stand, on this grassy land." The globe sped towards me until the UK had stretched out, its borders disappearing, the map surrounding me. It halted. Large yellow numbers hovered in my mind. Not wanting to lose the image, I kept my eyes shut.

A little out of breath from the magical exertion, I spoke into the phone. "I have the coordinates. Now what?"

"Are you okay?"

"Yes. I'm fine. It's kind of like going for a light jog. Don't worry. I have plenty of energy left."

Apprehension muted his tone. "Just making sure."

"So, now what do I do? We really should hurry." I cracked open one eye and cast a worried glance at the PIB building. Ma'am could be in there, unconscious right now. What if whatever the magic was had the ability to kill witches?

Will explained the next step. Damn. It was going to take a lot of power and concentration. If I got even one of the numbers wrong, they'd end up God knew where because there would be no anchor point in this spot. Random was not the way to go. They used to have mystery flights in Australia, where you could buy a plane ticket, but they didn't tell you where you were going. Many people found it exciting. I was pretty sure Will and Beren would not.

I shut my eye again, the shining numbers filling my mind. Now to do as Will had instructed.

I knelt and planted both hands on the cold ground. An earthy tang filled my nostrils. I syphoned as much of the magical river as I could, filling myself until it thrummed through every vein and pore. Then, as I pictured the coordinates and spoke the words Will had told me, I channelled the power into the soil. "Embed these coordinates into the ground, for thirty minutes, as a landing place easily found. When thirty minutes has expired, so too must the link to this place this spell provides." The ground heated beneath my palms and knees, steam rising. As the power leeched from my body into the thirsty soil, my fingers, arms, and shoulders ached. A cramp seized my stomach. Just when I thought I couldn't take anymore, it stopped.

Had it worked? I opened my eyes, gingerly stood, and stepped out of the circle.

Yes! The golden coordinates were embedded into the ground, glowing inside the circle. They slowly faded, until they disappeared. A surge of tiredness broke over me, and I resisted the urge to sit on the ground. I put the phone to my ear. "Done."

"Are you outside the circle?"

"Yes. It's safe for you guys to come through. I set it for thirty minutes." Any longer and other witches might have stumbled across it, which was a security risk, not that we weren't in the midst of one anyway, but why ask for more trouble?

"See you in a sec." Will hung up.

Within no time, Will emerged from his doorway inside the circle. His gaze met mine. He smiled, stepped out of the circle, and gave me a hug. "Great work, Lily."

"I do what I can. I'm tired though. That took a lot out of me."

"Temporary landing spots are harder the permanent ones. Now, tell me what happened."

As Beren stepped out of his doorway, I recounted the last fifteen minutes to Will. The alarm hadn't stopped wailing either. If it didn't stop soon, it was going to drive me mental. By the time I'd finished, Liv and Gus had joined us. Liv said, "Ma'am hasn't responded to my calls or texts. She's probably inside."

Will nodded and turned to Beren. "How are we going to do this?"

"Repel-magic spell?" Beren suggested.

Will blew a heavy breath out. "I was afraid that was going to be your suggestion. Okay." He made a bubble of silence. "We'll head to the control room and get that damned alarm turned off, then we go straight to the reception room, drag out everyone we can, starting with Ma'am. Once we've done that, we'll go back in and look for the source of the spell." Will turned to me. "You said you felt sick just from going near the door?"

"Yes. It was awful. Gus could hardly walk when he came out. Could you, Gus?"

"No, Miss Lily, I couldn't. It was like I'd drunk too many lagers, if you know what I mean. Couldn't walk straight, wanted to throw up. It was like the worst hangover ever."

Even though I was still tired, I had to ask, "Do you need me to come with you?"

Beren shook his head. "No. A repel spell is going to drain us. It's going to have to constantly repel the magic coming our way."

"Won't a return-to-sender spell work?" I wrinkled my forehead.

"No, but we don't have time to explain. Come on, Will." Beren turned and jogged towards the PIB, drawing his gun as he went. Will gave me a quick nod, then followed.

Liv and I shared a worried look and stared at the building. Beren's and Will's magic ruffled my scalp before they disappeared inside. I wandered closer.

"Lily," Liv warned.

I stopped. "I know. But I just—"

"No!" She caught up to me. "They'll be fine. The last thing they need is having to rescue an extra person."

I bit my bottom lip, and my shoulders sagged. "I know." Gah, it was so difficult to just wait. Doing nothing was not my strong suit. Liv and I stood shoulder to shoulder and waited.

After checking the clock on my phone twice in a minute,

Liv swatted my arm. "Stop! That's just going to make it take longer."

"At what point should I assume they need help?" Because, let's face it, I wasn't going to wait forever for them to emerge.

"Give them two more minutes to turn off the alarm. Once it's off, give them five minutes to get Ma'am down here. If they're not out by then, you can try going in. But you don't know that spell Will mentioned, do you?"

My enthusiasm waned. "No." Why was I so useless? Just when I thought I'd come so far, I realised I hadn't. Not even trying to control myself, I didn't just look at the time, I set a timer with an alarm set to go off in two minutes. Yes, I was an all-or-nothing kind of woman. As my timer counted down, I fixed my gaze on the exit.

The screeching alarm stopped.

It had rung for so long, its echo haunted my ears. "Has it really stopped?"

Liv placed her hands over her ears, then brought them down. "Yes, I believe it has." She grinned. "I told you they'd be okay. Before you know it, they'll be at that door with Ma'am in tow."

I wanted to believe her, and goodness knew I tried, but I set my phone timer for five minutes. She rolled her eyes. Sadly, I couldn't share her faith that everything would just work out.

That exit door became the most important thing in my world.

I folded my arms and hugged myself against the chill.

Please hurry up. I checked my phone. Two minutes and twenty seconds to go. It was amazing how an hour could fit into five minutes. At least, that's how it felt.

Now the alarm was quiet, the building appeared normal, no trace of the life-and-death struggle going on inside. Okay, so it might just be a life-and-vomit struggle, but still…. Someone had set off the alarm, cast the spell. Who and why? They obviously had a lot of power. What had stopped them outright killing everyone? If they could breach the PIB so easily, we should all be terrified. Was it Regula Pythonissam?

I was about to lift my coat sleeve and cast a disdainful eye on my unwanted snake tattoo, but my phone alert sounded.

Time was up.

I silenced my phone and looked up. Liv's worried eyes met mine. "Be careful, Lily."

"I will." Even though she didn't want me going, the man she loved was in there, and that was enough for her to give in.

I swallowed the lump of fear clogging my throat and set off. I'd meant to walk quickly, but my brain had other ideas, and I ran. I reached the door—dizziness returning from whatever that spell was—and grabbed the handle, but before I could pull it open, it swung outwards, bumping me out of the way.

Will stepped out, Ma'am cradled in his arms like a very big child. Her eyes were closed.

I stepped out of the way to give them room. "Is she

okay? Are you okay?" Beren followed Will out, Imani over his shoulder like a sack of potatoes. Will and Beren walked away from the building and laid them carefully on the grass.

Will pulled out his phone, made a call, and was off within a minute. "Lily, I'm calling other agents. We'll need help. There are six agents and fifteen non-witch staff inside that need our help. Beren and I are going straight back in. When the agents arrive in the circle, direct them to the building. Tell them we need two agents in the cafeteria, two to the reception room, and the rest, we need a sweep of the ground floor and basement levels. You got that?"

"Yes. Is there anything I can do for Imani and Ma'am?"

"Call James. Give him the coordinates for the landing spot. He's not the healer Beren is, but I'm hoping it's just the horrible effects of the spell that make you feel like you have the flu. There hopefully won't be any permanent damage."

"Come on, Will." Beren stood at the door, holding it open. His magic shone from him—the repulsion spell was obviously working hard to deflect whatever the attacking spell was. At that rate, he and Will would be lucky to last another ten minutes in there.

"Be careful," I said as Will followed Beren through the door. It clicked shut. I tried to focus on what I could do, so I dialled James and knelt in between Imani and Ma'am. Liv had joined us.

James picked up. "Hey, Lily. I'm just in the middle of something."

"I'm sorry, but we've got an emergency at headquarters. I'm outside and fine, but the alarm went off. There's some spell on the place, knocking everyone out. I have Imani and Ma'am unconscious out here on the grass. They need healing. I've set up a special landing place, but there's only about fifteen minutes left on it, and Ma'am and Imani really need help now. I'm going to send you the coordinates. Okay?"

"Hang on." James covered the phone. I couldn't understand the muffled noises. Finally, he came back to me. "Okay. I'll be there in a moment. Send those coordinates. Bye."

I concentrated on my brother and opened up to my magic, then imagined the coordinates flying through the cosmos to him. You could send thoughts that way or just think really hard of the person you wanted to contact, and imagine you were physically speaking to them or transferring a picture mind-to-mind. I supposed it was just the intent, but your magic needed to be clear on who you were sending to.

I gently patted Ma'am's cheek. "Ma'am, are you awake? It's Lily. Hello." Pat, pat, pat.

She groaned and opened her eyes. Thank God. Relief tumbled through me. She sat up. The movement must've brought on more dizziness because she held her stomach and slammed her eyes shut.

"Argh, what the hell happened?" Imani's weak voice came from behind me. I turned. She hadn't sat up, but she had a hand on her forehead, and her eyes were closed—the eternal position for someone suffering a hangover. Unfortunately, there'd been no fun getting there.

"We've been attacked, dear." Ma'am's snark couldn't be

subdued. I smiled. She was definitely going to be okay.

I explained everything that had happened since Liv had called her the first time. "And here's James." My brother strode from the landing spot, five agents on his heels. When he reached me, more came through their doorways. Seemed like we'd roused an army.

James knelt next to me and took Ma'am's chin in one hand, directing her to look straight at him. "I'm going to assess you now," he said. She gave a brief nod, and her skin took on a green tinge. That nausea was a killer.

The familiar warmth of my brother's magic trickled over me. The other agents ran past, donned protection spells, and stormed the PIB, guns drawn. A plethora of magic cascaded over me—it was like being doused with cold water. I shivered. It took a few moments to adapt to the sensation of that much power emanating from so many people.

James finished with Ma'am and turned to Imani, where he repeated whatever he'd done to Ma'am, who stood, straight and sure, back to her old self. That boded well for everyone else Will and Beren were going to drag outside.

Speaking of which, both men exited, each with a man slung over his shoulder. One looked to be a security guard, the other was one of the guys who served at the cafeteria. Ma'am called out. "Set them down here. James will see to them in a minute. Brief me. And drop the protections— conserve your energy."

Will and Beren did as asked, both breathing as if they'd run a sprint. Okay, so they had just simultaneously held a draining spell and carried men who weighed as much as they did. What did I expect? They were witches and agents, not superheroes.

Ma'am walked away, the men following. James had finished with Imani and was working on the cafeteria guy. Liv helped Imani stand. "Are you okay?" she asked.

"Yes. That was ridiculous. We landed in the reception room, wary because we knew the alarm had been activated. But our return-to-sender spells had no effect. Before we knew it, we were on the floor throwing up. I ended up passing out." She frowned. "Whatever that spell is, it's a doozy."

"How are they going to turn it off?" Liv asked.

Imani carefully shook her head. "I don't know. Either it's a spell unleashed in the centre of the building, set to pulse out power for a certain amount of time, or it's been integrated into the protective ward around the PIB, which would be pretty impossible. If someone had the know-how to do that, we'd be in massive trouble." My eyes must have radiated the horror because she was quick to continue. "But don't worry. That's pretty much impossible."

Hmm, bit too little too late. I totally needed something else to worry about. And, yes, that was sarcasm. I made a bubble of silence. "Do you think it's RP?"

"I don't know. The PIB has many enemies. We've put away some of the most psychopathic witches that exist. A powerful one with a grudge is just as dangerous as RP, and I can think of two or three that would have the resources on the outside to pull this off."

The PIB door opened, and one by one, agents emerged, carrying or dragging groggy and unconscious people. James had finished with everyone and motioned for the agents to lay them down near him. Boy, did he have a lot of work to do. Thankfully, Beren joined him. Ma'am must have reassigned him.

Will came over to Liv, Imani, and me. He magicked a clipboard with paper attached, and a pen to his hand, then passed them to Liv. "Can you please do a staff count? Mark off everyone who's out here, and who ends up out here. We need to see if we're missing anyone who was at headquarters when this started, and anyone who was called back. The names are already on there." He turned to Imani. "Get your name ticked off and go home."

Her eyes widened, and she planted her hands on her hips. I couldn't see her arguing with Ma'am like that, but Will was pretty much her equal as an agent. "But I'm all right. Agent Bianchi healed me. I'm ready to serve as needed."

"Ma'am's orders." Will wasn't having it, though. Imani scowled but said nothing further. Will looked at me. "Ma'am has asked that you go home for the rest of the day. She'll be home later to question you about what happened, but for now, you need to recuperate. And you did an exceptional job with the landing spot. Thank you."

Now I knew Will was okay, I wasn't going to argue about going home. The fewer people Ma'am had to worry about, the better. "Okay. I'll see you later. Stay safe." I smiled and made my doorway. Afternoon nap, here I come.

CHAPTER 2

After my three-hour nap, I got up and read for a while. I waited until seven, but Will and Ma'am were still at work. I texted Will to make sure they were okay. He responded to say they were staying until they could turn off the spell and secure the premises. That was two hours ago. I'd eaten dinner alone, and even though Ma'am wanted to question me when they got home, I despaired of that happening any time soon. I yawned, contemplating going to bed. Unfortunately, Liv was still staying at Beren's, after having to move out just in case the tattoo made me dangerous. It meant I was often home alone because Will and Ma'am worked such long hours.

Meh, there wasn't much going on, except me holding a pity party for myself. It was definitely time to go to bed. I could answer Ma'am's questions tomorrow. I stood from the chair in front of the fire—my favourite spot in the house—

and walked to the hallway. Just as I placed my foot on the first stair tread, the reception-room door handle rattled. Ooh, someone was home! It was sad how excited I was. I did my best not to jump up and down. Maybe I was turning into a dog.

Ma'am stepped through, followed by Will. I grinned. "Hello!" I bypassed Angelica—who wasn't on board with too much touchy-feely stuff, and, to be honest, I normally wasn't—and gave Will a massive hug. He brought out cuddly Lily. Totally mushy, but true. "How did it go? Did you work everything out? Do you want a cup of tea, something to eat?" Both of them had dark circles under their eyes —a sure sign they'd used way too much magic—and they weren't exactly smiling.

"A tea would be lovely, dear. Let's retire to the living room." Yes, it would've been easy for Angelica to magic herself one, but she'd used too much today, and she definitely needed a rest.

We took our places on the Chesterfields: Will and I sitting opposite Angelica. I magicked her a cup of tea and Will a cup of hot chocolate. Even though he hadn't asked for one, I knew he enjoyed them. They both thanked me as they sat back and relaxed, hot beverages in hand.

After drinking some of her tea, Angelica placed the cup back on the saucer on the low table between the couches. She sat up straight, as if she had all the energy in the world. I wanted to tell her it was okay if she was tired, that I wouldn't think any less of her and neither would Will, but I didn't. Maybe showing strength was her way of coping? It was probably better for all of us. If Angelica freaked out, it would be easy to believe we were doomed. She was the master at keeping us calm and thinking rationally, even in the worst situations.

Ma'am—which was how I thought of her when she had her serious face on—met my gaze. "Tell me what happened today. Everything from start to finish. Don't leave out any detail, no matter how minor you think it is. Oh, and would you mind"—she waved her hands about—"doing the honours?"

I nodded. Whatever they'd had to do at the PIB had obviously drained them completely. Happy to be able to help, even in such a small way, I made a bubble of silence, then recapped my day, starting with Imani and I covering the theft at the antique-furniture shop, to making the doorway landing spot, and feeling sick. I stopped at the moment I'd come home. And because I hadn't already done it, I texted Ma'am the photos I'd taken, showing the man who'd stolen the antiques.

She scrutinised the pictures and looked up at me. "Thank you for these, Lily, and for all your help today. You did well." She smiled.

Ooh, a compliment from Ma'am! A rare thing indeed. It warmed my chest, and I grinned. "Thank you. It was my pleasure. So, what happened with the spell? Did you manage to dissolve it? And do you have any idea why this all happened?"

Ma'am and Will looked at each other, poker faces intact. How they could decipher each other's guarded expressions was beyond me—wasn't that what the poker face was for? Making it hard for people to know what you were thinking? They were totally next level.

Ma'am gave a small nod, then said, "We managed to stop the spell, and, yes, we know the reason we were targeted… at least, part of the reason. We don't know who it was, as the signature isn't in our database, but it's the same magical signature that was at all of our call-outs today." She swallowed and licked her bottom lip. This wasn't going to be good. "The criminals, whoever they are, broke into one of our safes. It wasn't only protected with non-magical security, but we had spells on it. They stole three items."

So many questions popped into my brain in a whirl of fear. That was some feat to break through all that security. And what items had they taken? Were they things to use against us later? Were they things that would pose a national or international security risk? And lastly, was it the snake group? Were we about to lose the battle against them when we'd hardly started? "Was it RP? What items?"

"We don't know for sure, although, as I said, the magical signature wasn't in our database. They stole the ring Dana used to mask and increase her power. The other items were two bracelets that connect the witches wearing them, and they can share power, making them much stronger, and another ring made of platinum that a witch can put on another—witch or non-witch—and control their mind. All dangerous items that will make catching this person, or group of people, more difficult. We're leaning towards this being more than one person because the magnitude of the heist was too complicated. It seems the perpetrators have been planning this for a while, and all the jobs we were called out for today were to make sure there were as few agents as possible at the PIB so the major crime could be perpetrated. What their end goal is, we have no idea." She shook her head and pursed her lips. "There was one other clue. They left a short note that said, 'You made it too easy. Try and make it more fun next time. Oh, and gesundheit."

Huh? That was weird. "Is someone doing this for fun? Or is that just what they want you to think? And what's with the bless you?" Ma'am's subtle shrug was the only answer she gave. I sighed. I didn't want to ask—there was surely no good answer—but my curiosity won, again. "What do we do now?"

"We investigate it, of course." She looked at me as if I'd asked what my own name was. "I have agents working around the clock. The sooner we get those artefacts back, the better. We'll meet tomorrow at nine, but rather than the conference room, we'll convene in the PIB lecture hall."

"There's a lecture hall?" There was so much I didn't know.

"Of course, dear. How do you think agents learn everything they need to know? We have a gymnasium for the physical side, and lectures for the legal and operational side. There's also a spell-testing room."

"It sounds a bit like 007." I giggled. "Do your agents practice blowing stuff up with magic?"

. . .

Will grinned. "Yep. You should try it. It's loads of fun."

Ma'am rolled her eyes. "In any case, I need sleep. I have an insanely busy day tomorrow. I suggest you both get some sleep too. We're all going to need it. I'm sorry, Lily, but it's all hands on deck, and we definitely require your help."

"Okay. I'll be there tomorrow. I'm sure Gus or Will can show me where the lecture hall is."

Ma'am stood. "I'm sure they can. Goodnight." She gave a wan smile and walked out.

Will put his arm around me and pulled me into him. He sighed out a heavy breath, his voice low. "This is like nothing we've ever faced." He shook his head. "They made our defences look like crepe paper. I want you to have your return to sender up when you're in the PIB from now on."

"Um, okay, sure."

"I mean it, Lily. We can't afford to drop our guard at all." He looked at the ceiling and frowned.

"What?"

He turned his gaze on me. "The spells protecting this house and James's are going to need an overhaul. James and I are going to work on some tomorrow. We could use your help."

Huh? "My help? But I'm… I won't say *stupid*, but, you know, I'm not exactly top agent material. There's nothing I could come up with that you two couldn't."

He smiled. "That's where you're wrong. The spells we normally use are ones that have been used for generations. When you create a spell, there are many threads of magic that weave together. Normally, the magic dictates how that happens, and hence, spells are passed down through the ages via a grimoire, without any need to change them. To make magic easy to use, you just have to tell the magic your intent, and it will work out most of the rest for you, but it is possible to craft spells, weave the golden threads until no one can decipher them. But it takes time, patience, and a lot of energy. It's next-level stuff and not something every witch is skilled enough to accomplish."

"And we're sure RP can't spy on my magic while I have this thing on my arm?" I held up my arm, but my sleeve covered the offending tattoo, and I wasn't about to reveal it. The less I saw it, the better. It creeped me out. No matter how many times they said it was okay, they still couldn't prove it, and that worried me.

"Even if RP could tell whether you were drawing magic, there would be no way they could tell what you were doing with it. Okay?"

"Okay." Well, if anything happened because of it, I'd at least know I'd done my best to make sure everything was safe. Hmm, maybe there was a spell I could come up with that isolated my tattoo, cut off any kind of awareness it had, and cut off its ability to transmit information. I'd brought it up with Ma'am the other day, but she'd said it would take too much time and energy to devise something and then implement it, but if I was working on spells with Will and James, maybe I'd learn a few things I could use?

Will yawned. I smiled. "Time to get you into bed, mister."

"I need a shower first. What a day it's been." He stood. "Come on." He held out his hand, and I took it. Who would've thought we had anything to look forward to, but we did.

Bed.

CHAPTER 3

Will's alarm went off at eight, and we both got up. It was rare for us to go to the PIB at the same time. Having breakfast with him was something I usually only did on the weekends, so I actually woke up in a good mood for a change. I used the bathroom first, and when I was done, I went downstairs to make breakfast.

Angelica was already there, ready for work, sitting with her back to the door. My steps faltered as I entered the kitchen, and I stopped. What the hell?

Without turning to look at me, Angelica said, "Whatever are you doing, dear?"

"Um…" I walked around the other side of the table and sat to face her. "I just didn't expect you to change your hair colour. That's all." And only at the back. Her hair was greying and normally immaculate, but whilst the front and top of her hair was still that colour, her bun was hot pink. Funnily enough, it didn't diminish her aura of authority. But still, was she having a late midlife crisis?

Her brows drew down. "What are you talking about? I have too much to deal with today to suffer fools." Hmm, someone got up on the wrong side of bed today.

"Are you having a lend right now?"

"Whatever does that mean, having a lend?"

Gah, the language barrier between Australia and the rest of the world. "You know, are you joshing me? Unless there's something wrong with my eyesight, your bun is hot pink. Would I lie to you?" I tilted my head to the side and raised my brows. I was nothing if not honest, and being accused of fibbing really made me cranky. This was too much to deal with BC—before coffee. I mumbled the make-myself-a-cappuccino spell, and the coffee mug appeared in front of me, a few inches above the table. It crashed down with a loud clink-thud onto its side. Coffee splashed everywhere, then spilled across the table. What. The. Hell? At least I was still in my PJs.

"Was that to make a point, dear? If it was, you can stop with the histrionics."

My mouth dropped open. "Of course not! That was an accident." I stood and grabbed a sponge from the sink. I could've cleaned it up with magic, but sitting at the table staring across at Angelica was not good for my health while she was in such an ornery mood.

Will walked in. "Good mor—" He managed to get further into the room than I had before he halted.

I rinsed the sponge and wrung it out before continuing the clean-up. "Tell her," I said. "She doesn't believe me." Angelica pressed her lips together, obviously hating the fact that she was about to be proven wrong.

Will wrinkled his brow. "Doesn't believe you? But she would have done it." He came to my side of the table and looked at Angelica. "Why do you have a pink bun? I mean, it looks fine, but it's just surprising."

She growled. Yikes. She slammed her hands on the table, inadvertently landing in the coffee I hadn't yet wiped away. It splashed on her white shirt. I cringed. She stood, the force of her anger pushing her chair back so violently that it fell. Man, it was noisy in here this morning.

As Ma'am stormed out and up the stairs—hopefully to check that we were telling the truth—Will and I looked at each other. He raised a brow. I shrugged. "Don't ask me. She thought I was joking about her hair though, and I thought she was joking about me being joking." I shook my head. It was definitely too much to deal with BC.

"What happened here?" He flicked his gaze to the coffee disaster on the table. "Angelica didn't throw your coffee at you, did she?" He smirked.

I chuckled. "No, although the mood she was in, I'm lucky she didn't throw her teacup at my head. It was my stupid fault. I must've been distracted when I made my coffee spell. It didn't appear on the table but above it. I think I'm just tired."

His brows drew down. "That doesn't sound right. Unless you have practically no power left, that spell should just work. Even if you mumble, the magic knows what you want."

"Apparently, it wasn't listening very well today." I finished cleaning, rinsed the sponge out, and put it on the counter next to the sink. For safety's sake, I stayed at the sink and said my spell again, this time adding the condition that the cup had to appear safely and upright in the sink—if I managed to stuff it up again, at least the mess would be contained.

The cappuccino materialised, safe and sound in a mug in the ceramic bowl. Phew! I reached in and grabbed it, taking a sip to soothe my nerves. "Thank God that worked."

Will's magic feathered my scalp, and pancakes, jam, and cream appeared on the table, along with two plates and knives and forks. I smiled and sat. "Why, thank you, kind sir."

He grinned. "My pleasure, my lady." He took my hand and kissed it. Okay, so I giggled. I was such a sucker for a gentleman, especially if it was Will.

I grabbed two pancakes and smothered them in jam and cream. My mouth watered—although it was closed so I didn't hit anyone with my salivary excitement this time. I cut a piece and lifted the fork to my mouth. It smelled delicious. I popped it in. Mmm… I stopped midchew, gagged, and spat the pancake onto my plate. Oh my God!

Will glared at me. "What are you doing?"

I blinked and swigged some coffee. "'How much salt did you put in there' is not a question I should be asking of someone who just made pancakes. Are you trying to kill me?"

He gave me a what-the-hell-are-you-talking-about look and tasted it himself. His eyes almost bugged out of his head, but instead of spitting it out—he was too refined for that—he quickly swallowed and gulped down his own coffee.

Angelica appeared at the door, her poker face stubbornly in place. "We need to talk."

I started laughing. Oh, God, the more I looked, the worse it became. Tears sprang to my eyes, and I guffawed. Will, the cool guy he was, just smirked. "I didn't know you were a fan of Pikachu. If I'd known, I would've gotten you a Pikachu onesie for Christmas."

Angelica's jaw muscle twitched, and if looks could kill, we'd both have been cremated on the spot. But what did she expect our reaction to be? She'd changed her coffee-stained work shirt to a white T-shirt that had a joyful, smiling Pikachu on the front. I stopped laughing long enough to say, "The Pika slippers are a nice touch." The heat in her glare intensified, and I snorted. Oh, God, my stomach hurt. As I laughed, I held my hand to it.

"Enough!" she yelled. Nooooo! I couldn't stop laughing, and that had made it worse. I slid down my chair onto the floor. This was too much. Even Will couldn't hold it in anymore and was cracking up, his dimples making a good showing.

"Please?" Her plaintive tone brought me back to my

senses. I'd never heard that from Angelica before—it was shocking that she even knew how to convey that tone.

Wiping my arm across my face to remove the tears, I took a few breaths and clambered back into my chair. Setting eyes on that getup made me want to keep laughing, but I mashed my lips together and bit my tongue. She rolled her eyes. "For goodness' sake. Get over it. I'm wearing childish clothes. Big deal. Now, can you tell me why this is a problem?" Her voice was back to its normal bossiness. Still, the question risked setting me off again. I was going to let Will answer.

He schooled his expression until seriousness replaced mirth. The fun was over. "I take it you didn't intentionally make your hair pink or... the other... stuff." Thank goodness he didn't spell it out, or I'd surely be done for again. I shut my eyes, just in case, blocking out Angelica and her cute attire.

"No, I didn't, and as clumsy and inexperienced as Lily is at times, I've never seen her botch a simple spell—well, except for that one time when she was first here. The point is, making coffee is new-witch stuff." She just had to get that dig in there. Typical. Now I didn't feel so bad about laughing.

Will nodded. He rubbed his forehead. "My pancakes have too much salt, as in, an inedible amount. There's definitely something going on."

Angelica gave a firm nod. "Right. I'm going to go upstairs and get changed. Then we'll drive to the PIB. I'm not taking any chances."

Huh? "Are you saying that our magic's been... compromised?"

"Yes. I'll leave Will to explain it to you. I suggest you both go and get dressed. We'll need to leave ASAP since we can't travel to work. I don't want to be late." She turned and strode out.

I turned to Will. "Does that mean our bubble-of-silence spells won't work?"

"Not necessarily—some will work, and some probably won't. Someone—most likely whoever attacked us yesterday—has infected us with a confuse-magic spell, which comes under curses in witch lore. They're more than a simple spell. A curse, unlike a spell, will have continuing effects. A spell does whatever it does either right away or once, but a curse embeds in the witch's magic until a cure can be found or the spell unravelled, but it's tied off so it doesn't drain the witches power. It's created the same way a spell is, but with a twist, and it's way more complicated to set up, which is why they're not common. Does that make sense?"

"As much as it's ever going to. Is it easy to fix?" Magic was hard enough without it being super unpredictable. And we didn't need RP being privy to everything we said and did. Even if it wasn't them who'd done this to us, they would benefit from us turning into clumsy hacks.

"It may be, but it may not. I can explain in the car. We'd better get dressed. We don't want to keep Angelica waiting." He winked and stood, then frowned at the table.

"What's wrong?"

"Should I risk cleaning this up with magic?"

I sighed. "No. You might make a bigger mess. Come on —it won't take long." I grabbed the plate of pancakes and slid the salty mess into the bin before putting the plate in the dishwasher. Not using magic was going to be painful. I just had to hope it didn't last too long, especially since RP now had the upper hand.

I tried to put that out of my mind as I loaded cutlery into the dishwasher—I didn't need to stress myself into a frenzy. *Stay positive, Lily.* This had to be a record for how fast my day had devolved. Let's hope it didn't continue, or none of us would see tomorrow at the rate things were going. *Positive, I said.* But some things were easier said than done.

CHAPTER 4

Because of the new development, when we got to the PIB, Ma'am delayed the start of the meeting in the lecture hall. She wanted to liaise with James, Will, and a couple of other agents before she addressed everyone. The halls were teeming with agents in uniform. Even though they were short-staffed, they looked to have a healthy number of employees. I'd never seen so many agents in the building. I guessed that made sense since they all did shift work. Because everyone was busy, and I wasn't included, I decided to attempt breakfast again.

I found a table in the cafeteria to sit at and enjoy another coffee and a ham-and-cheese croissant. Most of the tables were full, for a change—likely others were in the same predicament we'd been in—magicking an inedible breakfast. Unlike in Costa, no one was laughing. Longing for the warm, vibrant café filled me. It had become part of my routine, and part of what it meant to be home and happy. How strange that your life could completely change, and within a few months, it became the new normal. Unfortunately, danger and wonky magic were today's new normal, and I didn't want to get used to that.

This issue was serious. How would they catch witch criminals without having reliable witch power of their own? And how vulnerable were my family, friends, and I to the whims of RP? The croissant wasn't giving me as much joy as it should with all the worry clouding my brain. What a waste of a flaky, yummy croissant.

This glitching of everyone's magic would also put a halt to figuring out and neutralising my tattoo. I shook my head. My "stay positive" mantra was not going to cut it today. I sighed and drank the last of my coffee. Thinking was not a good idea. Maybe I could read. Oh, nope. I hadn't brought my iPad, and I hated reading on my phone. There was no way I was going to try and magic my iPad to myself—I'd probably break it. Not having magic was way more of an issue than I'd ever realised…. I guessed I'd never really thought about it too much, or if I had, it was in extreme situations where I hadn't actually had a chance to miss it yet.

"Hey, Lily." Olivia sat opposite me.

I smiled. "Hey! How are you feeling today?" It was good to see my best friend. I missed living with her.

"I'm okay. A bit tired. How are you? Have you had any… accidents today?"

She must be referring to my magic. "Yeah. What did B

do?" He must've had an issue this morning since he was at the PIB yesterday.

She grinned. "It was hilarious. We're lucky no one else was around because he magicked his clothes on, and that was fine, but two minutes later, they disappeared, leaving him buck naked. We were just about to leave and travel here." She giggled.

My mouth dropped open. "Oh my God." I laughed. "That would've been funny."

"So what happened at your place this morning?" I recapped this morning's shenanigans, and she laughed. "Ha! Lucky Ma'am's wardrobe issues were just Pikachu related."

I snorted. "I do not want to see her naked. That would've been mortifying."

We laughed for a minute, and when she'd finally calmed down, she said, "It's been a madhouse since that breach yesterday. I assume you know they stole some things?"

I nodded. "Yeah. The whole thing's scary. If they're capable of that...." We looked at each other, neither of us willing to finish the sentence.

Someone shouted profanities. Liv and I sat up straight and jerked our gazes to the kitchen behind the counter. Crockery smashed on the tiled floor in there, and two chefs had run to the counter. Another crash came from the cooking area. The chefs looked at each other, one gesticulating. The word "Idiot" was also shouted. Magic tingled my scalp, then more magic. Looked like they were trying to get whatever it was under control.

Oh, crap.

I stood, my mouth dropping open. The two chefs ran around the counter to the café side because they were being pushed out of the way by a giant... omelette? I sniffed the air. Yep, it smelled like one, and it was yellow with bits of bacon, onion, and tomato visible in its giant pillowy folds. It was slowly consuming the kitchen and counter area. Oops, there went the cash register.

A more powerful burst of magic and the omelette stopped expanding, but it was still there. The taller chef put his hands on his hips and stared at the other chef, whose white hat was skew-whiff on his head. He folded his arms. "It wasn't my fault."

"I told you not to use magic after the bacon disaster this morning, and then there was the orange-juice flood. How many times do I have to tell you? No magic!"

Dong, dong, dong, dong. It was as if we were in the airport, and an important announcement was coming. The two chefs stopped their altercation and looked up at the speakers. Ma'am's voice filled the room. Oh, so it was an announcement. "PIB agents, your presence is now required in the lecture hall. The meeting will begin in five minutes. Don't. Be. Late."

Liv stood, as did everyone else in the cafeteria who wasn't already standing ogling the omelette catastrophe—no one wanted to incur Ma'am's wrath... sensible, really. People started filing out, and Liv and I followed.

The lecture hall was located on basement level one. Rather than having hundreds of people wait for the lift, security had propped open the fire exit doors. Liv and I took the stairs.

The large black door to the hall opened to the top and very left of the tiered seating, which cascaded over thirty rows towards the lower-level stage. The rows held twenty-two seats each. Dimly lit, it was like being at the movies. Liv led the way to one of the lower-level rows, and we nabbed seats in the middle. Low murmurs hummed in the large space as hundreds of agents in uniform took their seats.

Ma'am stepped onto the stage from between black curtains. She approached the lectern, which already had a glass of water on it. Situating herself behind the lectern, she tapped the microphone. Feedback squealed through the speakers. A roomful of groans told her what we all thought about that.

Her smirk was clear from where I sat. Typical.

Before Ma'am had to ask us to be quiet, the room hushed, such was her formidable presence. She nodded, satisfaction radiating from her face. "Thank you for joining me here today for this extraordinary PIB meeting. As agents, you've dedicated yourself to the betterment of the world and the upholding of justice. The PIB has put away thousands of criminals, but there are, unfortunately, always more. And none as formidable as those we now face. But as capable as they've been so far, we will prevail. As you may have heard, the frenzy of theft yesterday was orchestrated in order to virtually empty this building of agents. The ploy worked—three powerful artefacts were stolen from one of our safes, and any agent who had attended this site yesterday was infected with a confuse-magic curse spell." She paused and took a sip of water. "So, you may ask, how are we dealing with this security breach and compromise of our power? Any agents who have magic that is misbehaving is now on desk duties. There were some agents in the field on unrelated cases who were not called back yesterday. They remain uninfected and will stay with their cases. Two of our doctors who had RDOs yesterday are also unin-fected, and they are currently working to ascertain a cure. Until that cure is realised, I would ask everyone to refrain from travelling and using your magic in any way—we have enough trouble without adding to it." She wasn't wrong there, although that giant omelette could have fed a village of starving people. "In the meantime, you will await the announcement of your name over the loudspeaker. Once the cure is found, we will call you in one by one. As for dealing with these criminals, we are still working that out. Please get to any unfinished paperwork you have—make the most of your time in this building. If I have any research assignments for you, you will find them in your email as the day progresses. I'm not taking any questions. That is all."

She turned and left via the way she'd entered.

I looked at Liv. "But I have questions." Apparently so did everyone else because the conversation ramped up to a loud buzz. "Do they know who's doing this and why?"

"I doubt it, or she would've said. Come on; you can work in Mill's office with me."

"But I don't have anything to do."

"Well, you have to stay in case they call you for healing, and I could use the help. Do you mind?"

I smiled. "Not at all. I would love to help you, plus, I've missed you." Okay, I was beginning to sound like a broken record, or would that be CD? There wasn't even a modern equivalent now that we streamed everything. I'd just have to get over missing my best friend and enjoy whatever time we did manage to spend together.

When we reached Liv and Mill's office, Liv checked her emails. Ma'am had lots of work for her, so I helped. I started by compiling all the information we'd received on the crimes yesterday that had taken the agents away from headquarters. In a separate file, I put all the information on what had transpired at the PIB yesterday. When that was done, I started going through it all to sort the evidence into what we could use and what needed further investigation. Unfortunately, there wasn't a lot in my "know for sure" pile.

"Why the long face?" Liv asked.

"There's not much to go on." I stuck my bottom lip out.

She sat back from her keyboard and gave me her full attention. "So what do we have for sure?"

"The same magic signature was used at all the crimes, out there and here, and the signature isn't one on file. There have been no fingerprints, no actual sighting of who it was for sure, except for the photos I took, and they're inconclusive. We have the note he or they left Ma'am after stealing the artefacts. The paper is in testing, just in case it's special in any way; maybe they can track down where it came from. And that's it. Which is virtually nothing."

Not looking the least bit defeated, she asked, "And what else do we have to follow up on?"

"According to these notes, Ma'am's ordering video surveillance from all the places that were hit, although some have probably been wiped since whoever it was set up the spells. They could've arranged some of these thefts weeks ago. I don't know what the life of a dormant spell is, but they've obviously planned it this way. And the PIB had over fifty call-outs yesterday. That would mean there had to have been a lot of preparation, and there was no way they could've done that in one day—some of the places were twenty miles apart. That amount of travelling would drain anyone, let alone having the power left to cast all the spells."

Liv scrolled through her emails again. She opened a document from one. "According to this, James and Ma'am are compiling a list of everyone who's threatened the PIB in the last ten years, and they're also going to question some of the more powerful criminals they've locked up over the years. This could take forever."

"And what's their end game? Is it just to beat the PIB, or are they planning some massive crime?" The options were frightening, especially if we couldn't break the curse affecting most of the PIB agents.

Liv shook her head and bit her bottom lip. She stayed that way for a while, then pursed her lips and sat up straight. "Whatever it is, we'll figure it out. Come on; we've got work to do."

I didn't share her confidence, but I did as she asked because this crime wasn't going to solve itself.

CHAPTER 5

I ended up working with Liv all day because I couldn't travel home, and I had to wait for Ma'am and Will to finish. Will and James had abandoned the idea of creating new home-protection spells as well, since anything we tried would be likely to fail or create havoc. Now that I'd done everything I could for Liv, I was standing at the window, staring out into the drizzling, gloomy afternoon. I didn't think I'd ever get used to it getting dark so early.

Liv's desk phone rang. She answered it. "Hello, Olivia speaking." She waited while the other person spoke for a minute. "Okay. Yes. Right away. Bye." She clicked the phone back on the hook. "Lily, that was Will." I turned to look at her. "He wants you to go down to the basement now and meet him and Ma'am at the car. They have to rush out to an assignment, and they're going to drop you home."

"Oh, okay. Well, it's been lovely spending the day with you." I smiled.

"It has. When this disaster is over, we should have a day in London shopping or something."

Shopping wasn't my favourite thing, but hanging out in London with my best friend sounded awesome. "Count me in." I grabbed my coat from the back of my chair. "See you later."

"Bye."

I made my way downstairs, past dishevelled agents, faces pinched in what I assumed was frustration. Waiting in the car were Ma'am in the driver's seat and Will sitting next to her. Wisps of hair had come loose from her bun. Her usual immaculateness must be a result of magic rather than a natural ability to remain impeccable all day. That gave me satisfaction as I opened the back door and slid into the seat behind her. She wasn't so perfect after all. Okay, so that was a little mean of me, but she liked to lord it over everyone, but she was, at the heart of things, just like everyone else. I shut the door.

"Gloat while you can, Lily, because once we have our powers back, I shall be immaculate once again. And I'm not like everyone else—I'm infinitely better." She smirked, gave a wink in the mirror, and started the car.

I groaned. "How can you still mind-read if you can't use your power?" Because we were told to drop our magic, I hadn't been able to use my mind shield, and she was back to her old tricks.

"Yes, I am back to my old tricks. It's one of my natural talents, and it seems as if this spell hasn't affected it."

"That's fantastic! Do you know if it's the same for everyone?"

Will turned to look at me as Ma'am negotiated the car park towards the exit. "We were going to see if you could use your talent and let us know. We'll do it at home, but first, we have to attend a crime scene."

"Why am I going with you?"

Will turned back around as the roller door opened to let us out. "Until we know whether or not RP is involved, you're not safe at home by yourself. If they can break through the spells we had protecting those artefacts, they have the ability to break those spells too."

"So we're pretty much sitting ducks right now?" As Ma'am pulled out into the compound and headed for the gate, silence permeated the cabin. Fear skittered around my stomach, and I shivered. We didn't have proper magic, so we couldn't attack or put up a return to sender. "But you guys have your guns, right?"

"Yes," Will answered, looking straight ahead. "Old school."

"Old school is better than nothing, I suppose." Yep, there was my positive streak coming out. Ma'am turned right into the street, heading for the main road. "Where is this crime scene, and what happened?"

Will and Ma'am shared a quick look before Ma'am flicked her gaze back to the road and said, "We'll tell you when we're there. The witch at the house hasn't had their magic restricted. She can make a bubble of silence for us. But don't worry, there's nothing gory."

That was a relief. "How were you discussing things at work today without the B.O.S."

"Do you have to do that, dear?"

"What? Shorten things?"

"Yes."

I grinned. "Yes. It's way easier." She shook her head.

Will watched the road ahead and answered, "We had someone who hadn't been in yesterday come and do it for us, but we sent them home quickly, just in case the infection could still take. We had them protect one room, which has become the hub of our operations for now. It's the control room you helped out in when we had all that trouble from the tea." That was a nice way to say the trouble caused by Piranha and RP.

I wanted to ask more questions, but considering anyone could be listening, I shut my mouth and looked out the window, although there was nothing much to see in the rainy darkness. Five felt like 7:00 p.m.

Eventually Ma'am turned into a country lane, and fifty metres down the road, pulled into the driveway of a neat brick bungalow. She parked next to a Volvo 4WD. "Am I coming in too?" At the risk of getting out of the car and being told to get back in, I figured I'd ask first.

"We want you with us, dear. It's not safe out here." Ma'am turned off the car and got out. Way to instil confidence. My shoulders tightened, and an ache pulsed at the base of my skull. Just what I needed. I hopped out and walked just behind them, seeing as they were the investigating agents, and I was just along for the ride. The cold air drew goosebumps along my arms, even though they were covered, and I dipped my head, trying to avoid the frigid raindrops.

Thankfully, Will and Ma'am were fast walkers, and we were soon under the cover of the front porch. Will rang the bell, and a young blonde woman answered the door. She was about my height and slim, her pretty face showing relief at seeing Ma'am and Will. "I'm so glad you're here. Andrew said you'd make it a priority. Thank you."

Ma'am went in first, then Will stepped back to let me go ahead of him while introducing me. "This is Lily. She works with us."

I smiled and held out my hand for her to shake. "Hi."

She took my hand. "Hi, Lily. I'm Kelly. Come in." Kelly led us through to her bedroom. Ma'am and Will followed her all the way to her built-in wardrobe. I stood just inside the doorway and folded my arms. I wasn't a prude, but being in a stranger's bedroom was weird and uncomfortable. A huge framed photograph hung above the bed. My eyes widened, and I looked away. Sheesh, some people were way too confident to have strangers coming into their room and seeing a photo of them with their significant other in lingerie. In the picture, Kelly had on a red lace number, and who I assumed was Andrew wore tight black briefs which left little to the imagination and a lot to see, which I couldn't un-see. Damn it. I peeked up at it again. Okay, so I was curious. Oh my, was that Kelly's nipple? I looked away and to the trio at the wardrobe and blushed. I really hadn't needed to know what Kelly looked like under her clothes, and if I ever ran into Andrew, I was probably going to blush and giggle. Why couldn't I be more of an adult?

"And that's everything?" Will asked, putting his notebook and pen back in his pocket. Oh, I'd missed it all. I hated myself sometimes. Why couldn't I just pay attention? Now I'd have to wait until we were in the car to ask what had been taken. I was my own worst enemy.

Kelly frowned, sadness in her eyes. "No. They took Benny, our beagle."

Ma'am's poker face stayed put. "Are you sure he didn't just escape by himself?"

She shook her head. "Definitely not. He can't jump, and there's no way for him to get out of our back garden or the house, and since they came in with magic and left the same way, no doors were opened, at least that I could tell."

"Did they leave a note?" I asked before I could stop myself. Ma'am scowled at me, probably for interrupting and sticking my nose in where it wasn't needed. Oops.

Kelly nodded. "Yes. But it didn't say anything about Benny, just that we could thank the PIB for the things that were taken. Andrew's already given it to Agent Bianchi."

Ma'am folded her arms and gave me an extra cranky look for good measure. "Yes, and Agent Bianchi has passed it onto me. Thank you, Kelly." Right, so I was going to shut up now.

Kelly walked towards me, leading Will and Ma'am out, so I hurried into the hallway first and stood to the side, to get out of the way. Ma'am stopped in front of me and faced Kelly. "Agent Smith said he'd done some preliminary investigation when you first discovered things were missing, but do you mind if we have a look around?"

"Yes, that's fine. Andrew said you'd probably do that. Feel free. I'll just be in the kitchen. If you need anything, let me know." She smiled and headed off through another doorway. From the conversation, Agent Smith was probably Andrew, her partner or husband, or whatever.

Ma'am turned to me and gave a nod. Huh? I lowered my voice. "You want me to take photos?" She nodded. I was about to argue that my magic was off, as she very well knew, but then I remembered that it was my talent, which meant it probably wasn't affected. "Okay. I'll try. What did they take?"

"Family heirlooms worth a few thousand pounds. Gold, diamond, and ruby jewellery."

I pulled out my phone, because I couldn't magic my camera to myself, and headed back to the bedroom. I stood in the doorway and pointed my phone towards the wardrobe. Opening my portal to the magic river, I whispered, "Show me who stole Kelly's jewellery."

A figure in a long, black coat and balaclava. Great. They weren't giving us anything to go on. I took a photo, then walked around, taking photos from every angle. The one thing I could tell: this person was a tad shorter than the man in the antique store, maybe by three or four inches. I stood where they had been standing. "Will, can you take a photo of me, please?"

"Whatever for?" Ma'am asked.

"Trust me."

She shrugged, and Will, curiosity in his gaze, took my phone and stood back, pointing at me. I stood straight and looked at the phone. The phone made two click sounds, then he handed it back. "Done."

"Thanks. I'm comparing my height with theirs." I wasn't going to say any more—they'd know what I meant, but anyone listening in wouldn't.

Ma'am nodded slowly. "That's actually quite a good idea, Lily." If only she hadn't sounded so surprised. "I'll be back in a minute." She went through the door Kelly had just used. She must be going to tell her we were done. I turned to Will. "Aren't you going to look for anything else?"

"No. Our magic isn't working, and Agent Smith, Kelly's husband, dusted for fingerprints and conjured the magic signature earlier."

"Is it the same one we got from the other crimes?"

"I believe it's not. But it's still not in the system, so whoever it is, is a mystery."

Ma'am returned with Kelly. "Thanks for coming and having a look," Kelly said.

"It's our duty." Ma'am smiled. "If we find out anything further, we'll be in touch."

"Thanks." Kelly opened the door. "Nasty weather. Drive safely, Agent DuPree."

"I will, thank you." Ma'am was almost to the car by the time Kelly shut the door, and I stepped off the porch.

I ran through the rain to the car, jumped into the back

seat, and slammed the door. We had no magic with which to dry ourselves—well, we did, but the way that spell worked, we'd probably end up even wetter, or naked, or something equally undesirable. I clicked my belt in as Ma'am started the car. "Do you think we could have the heater on?"

"It's not that cold, dear." Easy for her to say. She was used to near-zero temperatures. I was a softy from Sydney, where even in winter, it rarely went below ten Celsius.

"Pretty please with sugar on top? I'm freezing." To emphasise the point, I wrapped my arms around myself and shivered.

Ma'am rolled her eyes. "Honestly, the things I do for you people." She turned the heater on and carefully backed out of the driveway.

Will smirked—I could see him in the side mirror—and I smiled. "Thank you." I was sure her grouching was for show… at least, I hoped so.

Will asked, "Lily, can you pass me your phone? I want to check out the photos."

"Sure." I unlocked it and handed it to him. "Should we go to any of the other places the crimes were committed so I can get photos?" Since my talent was still working, we might find a decent clue.

"Not at this stage, dear. With everything as it is, we don't want to risk more than we have to." She must have meant that because our magic was haywire, we couldn't protect ourselves properly, but, of course, we didn't know who was listening in. Although, we could probably assume RP knew what had happened. They likely had some kind of spy in the PIB, and that's even if the attack hadn't been them in the first place.

I stared out the window. *Oh, look, cows.* I breathed a quiet "moo." It was impossible to resist. The herd stood at the edge of a field at the fence line, which happened to be next to a street light. Were they cold out there in the winter rain? Why didn't they give them coats to wear like they did horses? Man, it would be terrible to be a cow, standing around all the time in that weather. And if they wanted to sit down, it would be onto the wet, muddy ground. Yuk.

"Lily? Hey, Lily!" I started. Will was twisted around, his arm bent weirdly as he tried to give my phone back.

"Oops, sorry." I grabbed my phone and held it in my lap.

He laughed. "Always off with the fairies."

"And the cows." I grinned. "It's better than thinking about what's going on. We need more clues."

"Well," Will said, "what you did today is a start. It will be tinily helpful, which is way better than not helpful at all."

"Tinily? That's not a word, but it should be. Welcome to my world!" I laughed. The serious old Will was becoming sillier. Maybe my good influence was making a difference.

"You are making a difference, dear, but I don't know whether it's good." Ma'am's smirk reflected in the rear-view mirror. Damn mind-reading talent. A grin replaced her smirk. It was my turn to eye-roll.

Will's phone rang. He pulled it out of his pocket and answered it. "Hey, James. What's happening?" Will listened, then said, "Okay. We'll meet you at Ma'am's. See you in twenty. Bye."

"What was that about?" I could never not know. The suspense would just about kill me.

"Your brother's meeting us at Ma'am's soon, but I can't tell you the why right now."

I sighed. "Fair enough." I bet Ma'am knew, though, since she could mind-read. I was always the last to know....

The rest of the car trip was filled with the swoosh of tyres through water and the rhythmic *thump, thump, thump* of the windscreen wipers. Tension strained my neck. It was as if I was waiting for something bad to happen. In light of everything that had transpired, we'd never been more vulnerable. If RP decided to attack now, the outcome wouldn't be good for us, unless our magic accidentally did something awesome we didn't expect. I supposed just because it was going haywire didn't mean the result would always be bad for us. Thankfully, we were just about home.

Ma'am pulled into our driveway. "That depends on the spell, dear. If the caster of our curse has made it so our spells do something negative for us each time, then that's what will happen."

"But there's negative, and there's *negative*. You wearing a Pikachu T-shirt wasn't all that bad, neither were Will's salty pancakes. We're lucky they didn't make every spell turn and kill us."

"That would be very difficult to achieve. Magic is neutral, and it would be very hard to make magic turn on its caster. The more negative you want the outcome to be, the more power it takes. And considering the caster has spelled so many of us, they would have had to spread their energy around. It wouldn't have been easy to accomplish everything they have so far, let alone make it stronger and more dangerous."

"Oh, okay." I had to take her word for it because I had no other point of reference. I hoped she was right and not just saying it to make me feel better.

"Would I really bother about trying to make you feel better, Lily?" she asked. Gah, mind-reading.

I shrugged. "I suppose not. You're more of a realist."

She smiled, although it was somewhat grim. "That I am. Now let's get inside."

As we exited the car and made our way to the front door, my brother's car pulled up behind Ma'am's in the driveway. Had I ever seen him drive over here? Normally we all travelled everywhere, and if there was driving to do, Will usually did it because his Range Rover fit everyone.

Ma'am opened the front door, and we filed in after her. I left the door open for James, who hurried inside, Millicent's dad, Robert, behind him. I gave James a quick hug, then looked at Millicent's dad. "How are you?"

"Well, thank you, Lily. How are you?"

"Good, thanks." I turned to James. "How's Mill and my gorgeous niece?" Thankfully, Millicent hadn't been caught up in this stupid drama, because she was still on maternity leave.

He grinned. "They're great, thanks. I've had her parents come over and help strengthen the protection spells on the house. Her mum had some in her family grimoire that haven't been used for years—they're particular to a village in the northeast. We think that'll do the trick." He nodded at Millicent's dad.

"It should do," he said. "They've fallen out of use because they were unnecessarily sturdy. They take a few hours to a day to put together, and they require patching every week, but they're much better than what witches use today. Like anything, standards have fallen. Things aren't what they used to be." I tried not to grin. Spell standards had fallen. Oh dear. James looked at me and subtly winked.

"Well, come on through." I shut the front door and ushered them through to the living room. "Have a seat. I would guess that Angelica's gone to make some tea. We'll be back in a moment. Do you want any?" My breath plumed in the cold. We hadn't been home all day, and the central heating had been turned off. I glanced at the fireplace, which, of course, was devoid of flames. If I wanted to light it, I'd have to do it the non-witch way.

"That would be lovely, thank you." Robert sat on one of the Chesterfields next to James.

"Nothing for me, thanks." James smiled.

"Okay. Be back in a minute." I made my way to the kitchen where Angelica was making tea the normal way, and Will was making nachos. "Can we have an extra cup of tea for our guest?"

"Since when does your brother drink tea?" Angelica asked.

"He's brought Millicent's dad with him. They're here to talk about the home-protection spells."

"Oh, lovely. I thought it would just be James. It's a good thing we can access witches who haven't been cursed." Ma'am took a tray out of the cupboard and placed two saucers, teacups, a bowl of sugar, and small milk jug on it while she waited for the kettle to boil.

"Does anyone need any help?" It was rare to see Angelica and Will do things in the kitchen the non-witch way. I'd only been out of normality for nine months, and just watching without helping wasn't the way I'd been brought up.

Will sprinkled cheese on corn chips and salsa, then turned to me and smiled. "No thanks. We're fine. Go chat to our guests, and we'll bring everything out when it's ready."

Guilt sat on my shoulder, dangling annoying legs that swung back and forth, kicking my bicep. *Give me a break. I've offered. They said no.* Kick, kick, kick. Grrr. I needed to get out of my own head. "Are you sure?"

The kettle whistled. Angelica turned it off and poured the water into the teapot. "We're fine. Now go. I'll be out with this in a moment."

Flicking the annoying passenger off my shoulder, I returned to the living room. "Tea will be here in a moment." I sat on the Chesterfield opposite my brother. He and Robert appeared to be discussing the pros and cons of a certain spell. Soon Will and Angelica came in. Will sat next to me, and Angelica sat next to him. "Um, can I ask a favour, Robert?"

He smiled. "Why, of course."

"Can you light a fire in the fireplace over there? I'm freezing, and, well, it would be easier than me having to bring in some firewood, etcetera."

Will scowled. "Why didn't you tell me you were cold? I'd have gotten the wood."

"You were busy." It didn't surprise me that Will didn't think of lighting the fire, or notice it was bloody freezing. Typical English folk. Magic tingled my scalp—calm, sensible magic. A *whoosh* came from the fireplace, and there it was: a big, beautiful, hot, glowing fire. I grinned. "Thank you!" Robert smiled, and I stood. I had to defrost my freezing hands.

While I warmed myself in front of the fire, Robert cast a bubble of silence. Then the more experienced witches discussed their plans for protection spells around the house. I listened intently—one never knew what awesome things they'd learn, and there was so much to know. Finally, my name was called.

"Lily, dear, would you mind coming back here?"

I made my way over and plonked myself onto the couch next to Will. "At your service." I smiled.

James looked at me. "Lily, would you mind showing Robert your tattoo?"

I held in a sigh. Those times when I'd forget about that marking were the better times, and the last hour was definitely a better time. I had no idea where he was going with this, but I stood, took my coat off, and pushed up my jumper sleeve. Leaning over the table slightly, I held my arm out in front of Millicent's dad.

He looked at it, then up at me. "Do you mind if I touch your arm?"

How polite. "That's fine." I smiled.

His cool fingers slid across the tattoo. He gently grabbed my wrist and turned my arm over, exposing the rest of the snake. "Hmm." Was that a good hmm or a bad one? It was like being at the doctor's. "I'm going to prod at it with magic. Is that okay?"

I shrugged. "Yep. Fine. Magic away." I had nothing to lose, except that stupid tattoo.

The magic normally only tingled on my scalp, but the sensation travelled down to my shoulder, arm, and the tattoo. After a couple of minutes, the magic stopped. Robert released my arm and looked up at me. "Lily, I think I can contain the tattoo and get rid of the tracking part of it."

I sucked in a breath. "You could really do that?"

His smile was kind. "I spent years in the army as a doctor. Only retired last year, in fact. I was privy to many powerful and intricate spells that aren't floating around in the wider world. I recognise the… style, if you will, of the spell's composition. Given enough time, I'm sure I could figure the whole thing out. But it's going to take a lot of time. The tracking is the easiest part to decipher. The masking spell is one that, as you work your way through the spell and get it right, it reveals more and more of the threads of the spell. The tracking one should take me a day or two of constant work. We have some other spells to get through on this house tomorrow, but I should have the energy to do it in, say, three days' time? Could you make yourself available? We could meet at James and Millicent's place."

Excitement spiralled through me. If we could ditch the tracking spell, and once the curse was fixed, I could keep going with research into my parents' disappearance. I bit my lip, hoping with every fibre of my being that he really could do what he said. "Yes, I totally could make myself available. You have no idea how happy I'd be if you could disable this thing." I held my arm up and glared at the snake. How much longer would I have to live with it? My shoulders sagged. Maybe I shouldn't even think about that.

Millicent's dad nodded slowly. "Splendid. I can't guarantee anything, but I'm pretty confident we can figure this out, Lily. See you in a few days."

"See you then." I smiled, but it was forced. What if he couldn't do what he thought he could? I guessed I'd just have to wait and see.

CHAPTER 6

The next morning, Angelica and Will drove to the PIB, and Millicent's dad returned with Millicent to spell the house. Thankfully, she hadn't been caught up in the curse. Her mum was at her place, minding the baby. Even though this was all good news, melancholy stung my eyes and sat heavy on my chest. My parents had missed out on this—meeting their granddaughter. And Annabelle had missed out on having the love and guidance of two wonderful grandparents. Someone had stolen this from our family, and I wasn't going to stop searching until I found out what had happened and who was to blame. What I'd do then, I didn't specifically know, but it involved pain and suffering for the guilty party.

While they did that, I stayed in my bedroom and read, then did a forty-minute workout from YouTube. I hadn't been running much lately because of everything that had been going on, and now we didn't have reliable magic, so everyone who'd been affected, including Will and Beren, had been forbidden to spend time away from home or PIB headquarters. The only time Will and Beren got to go anywhere was if an unaffected agent accompanied them to interviews. They had a lot of work to do to come up with a list of witches who wanted the PIB out of action. And even then, they didn't know if it was someone with a grudge or just someone who wanted to commit major crimes and not get caught.

Just after 4:00 p.m., someone knocked on my door. "Come in," I said from my spot on my bed where I was reading.

The door opened, and Millicent poked her head in. "Hey. Just wanted to let you know we're done." She smiled, came in, and sat on my bed, then sighed. The darkness under her eyes hadn't been there when she'd arrived this morning, and I'd been bombarded with magic sensations all day. Her dad must be exhausted too.

"Thanks for doing that. You look like you could use a good nap."

"More like a two-day sleepfest. But at least it's done. You'll be safe here now. How are you feeling?"

I shrugged. "I'm fine. That thing with the curse doesn't make me feel sick or anything, but I'm bored and frustrated. There's so much I can't do while my magic is compromised."

"With a bit of luck, they'll have a cure sorted in the next few days. I'm actually coming back to work while this is going on. I start back tomorrow. Mum's going to take care of Annabelle. They're staying at our place for a while, until we catch whoever's done this."

"Are you happy to be going back?"

She grinned. "Yes. As much as I love staying home and being a mum, the baby's been sleeping through, and I'm not really tired. I do miss adult company, and you know I love my work, so, yeah, I'm happy. And it's only until this stuff gets fixed; then I'll drop back to part-time. I'm thinking three days per week. Ma'am's too short-staffed, and working a few days a week is the perfect compromise."

"Sounds good. It'll be good to have you back… not that I'm always there, but I seem to be there a lot more than I'd envisaged."

She laughed. "You're just indispensable."

"Ha! I wouldn't quite say that. They really need to put more people on." I frowned. "I feel like we're never going to get to the bottom of RP, if you know what I mean. We just haven't got time to spend on it anymore."

She patted my knee and gave me a sympathetic look. "Don't worry, Lil. Things will get back to normal soon."

I raised an eyebrow. "Since when is anything around here ever normal?"

She grinned. "Okay, you got me there. Anyway, the house is all good, and we've woven an extra bubble of silence. It's only going to last for seven days because it just takes too much power to maintain, but if you still need it after that, we'll do another one. So feel free to say what you want while you're home." She stood. "I'm going to get going. Dad's already left, but he said for you to come visit the day after tomorrow for the tattoo." She bent down and gave me a hug, then stood.

"Great. I'll see you guys then. And thanks for today. I feel much safer now." I hadn't slept very well the last two nights. Feeling vulnerable wasn't pleasant. Even though I normally feared RP when I was out and about, I had magic I could use, but now that it was dodgy, I felt like the sole chicken at a party full of foxes.

"Bye." Mill waved, then stepped through her doorway and disappeared.

An hour later, I wandered downstairs to cook dinner. Having to prepare early was something I'd gotten out of the habit of. When you could click your fingers and have something at a moment's notice, there was nothing to think about beforehand. I checked the fridge to see what I could cook. Milk, cheese, and tomatoes, that was it. Oh dear. Maybe we'd have to get home delivery.

The front door slammed, the echo making it to the kitchen. I spun around to angry voices in the hall heading my way. My heartbeat spiked but slowed when I recognised Will's and Angelica's voices. What were they arguing about?

Angelica entered the kitchen first, her hand waving above her head in a "shoo" motion. "You know I did the right thing, William." Ooh, she'd used his full name.

Will came in after her, his grey eyes as dark as a stormy ocean in the late afternoon. The intensity of his gaze was more like a hurricane. What in the hell had happened? "You're not supposed to use your magic, dammit! We'll take your car tomorrow." He folded his arms.

Ma'am shook her head. "You're such a child. If I hadn't done anything, we would've hit that dog and killed it. Do you want that on your conscience?" He grumbled under his breath. "I thought so." A self-satisfied smile found its way to her lips.

Well, the suspense was just about killing me. "What happened?"

Will looked at me, a massive frown ambushing his face. "Angelica ruined my beautiful car."

She rolled her eyes. "It's only temporary, for goodness' sake. You men are such babies when it comes to your cars." She turned to me. "What's for dinner?" Wow, she was changing the subject way too quickly for my liking. I wanted to know more.

"Um, there isn't much in the fridge. I was thinking home delivery?" I walked to the door.

"Where are you going?" Will asked.

"To look at your car, of course." Will pinned Angelica with an angry glare. Silence engulfed the room as I turned. I guessed I'd have to see what the damage was for myself. How bad could it be?

I turned the outside light on and opened the front door to a blast of cold wind and drizzle. Ah, the joy of English weather in winter. I snuggled further into my jumper and stepped outside. Angelica's car sat in the driveway just near the front door. Will's car should be behind it. But the black roof that was normally visible above her car was nowhere.

I moved down the driveway. Once I reached the front passenger door of Angelica's car, the problem became evident. Oh. I pressed my lips together to keep from laughing.

A yellow rubber-ducky car perched in the driveway.

Was that even legally allowed on the road? It was a yellow duck, its body about the size of a Fiat, the head rising from the roof. I walked around it. The windscreen was in the chest of the bird. I snorted, picturing Will hunched over in the driver's seat, carried along by this cute ball of yellow, bumping over potholes as if it were waddling. Oh my God! What would happen if I honked the horn? I giggled and opened the driver's door—it wasn't locked, probably because Will figured no one would steal it. Maybe he even wanted someone to take it away.

I bent low and slipped my hand over the horn, pressing down three times. "*Quack! Quack! Quack!*" I burst out laughing and dropped into the seat. Tears streamed down my face. I pressed the horn again. "*Quack! Quack!*"

I couldn't hear anything over my hysterical laughter, so Will had managed to sneak up on me. He stood at the door, arms folded, staring down at me with the most disdainful face ever. "Are you quite finished?" A fresh round of guffawing took hold. The poor guy was so serious, but how could anyone be serious when they were driving a duck? My cheeks were wet, my stomach sore.

I finally calmed down enough to talk. "Can we keep it? It's so cute!" I snorted. Oops.

"I want my Range Rover back. This car is ridiculous."

I patted the dashboard. "Don't speak that way about my new friend. Maybe we should name it?"

"Get out of the car, Lily."

Hovering my hand above the horn, I stared at Will. His eyebrows drew down, and his lips pressed together. Smirking, my hand descended. "*Quack! Quack! Quack!*" The laughing recommenced. Will reached in and grabbed my arm, firmly but not too hard. He carefully extricated me from the car and shut the door, and there was nothing I could do because my mirth had incapacitated me. He led me to the house and inside, slamming the front door. By the time we reached the kitchen, I'd managed to take a few breaths and wipe my tears.

Angelica was grinning, her eyes crinkling at the corners. "The horn is a nice touch, don't you think? I'm rather proud of that feature, even though I didn't actually mean for it to happen."

"It's my favourite part of the car. You know, the world would be a much happier place if everyone had duck cars. Driving would be so much more fun."

"You make a good point, dear. Maybe you should write to some of the car companies, see if they can accommodate your wishes."

"I'll put it on my to-do list."

Will sat at the table and refolded his arms. Grumble bum. "I'm glad you two find this so damn hilarious, but I want my car back. No self-respecting agent drives a car that looks like that." He shook his head. "I can't even ask someone to fix it because I'd be the laughing stock of head-quarters."

I rolled my eyes. "You're far too sensitive. Get over it. It's just a bit of fun. I assure you, it doesn't affect your manhood in any way." I waggled my eyebrows, then laughed.

"This is where I stop the conversation." Angelica sat down. "No more talk about William's manhood, thank you."

"I'll second that," said Will.

"You people are no fun." I sighed loudly for effect.

Three paper bags appeared on the table. I jerked back. Bloody unexpected food arriving by Witcheroo. Except, I was hungry, so I wasn't going to complain. Angelica grabbed one bag, opened it, and looked at me. "I took the liberty of ordering dinner. Would you mind getting some plates, dear?"

I stood. "Of course." I did as asked, plus grabbed cutlery and returned to the table, placing everyone's settings in front of them. I inhaled. "Mmm, so, what yumminess did you get?" I sat and checked out the offerings. Barbecue chicken, baked vegetables, and garlic bread. "Thanks, Angelica. This looks delicious."

We all tucked in, and Will settled down after the ribbing we'd given him. My mouth curled up on one side. I'd needed that laugh after the week I'd had so far.

After dinner, we all cleared the table. I washed up while Will dried, then Angelica made tea, and we adjourned to the Chesterfields in the living room. By Angelica's serious face, we were likely about to discuss PIB stuff. "Yes, dear, that's exactly what we're going to do."

Damn mind-reading. "Can't you turn it off?"

"I can protect myself against other people's thoughts, which I normally do for non-witches, but it takes magic, magic I don't want to use. It's my talent, which means I can use it without making a spell, but I can't block it unless I cut off my magic, or I use a specific type of mind shield." I frowned. "Sorry, but it is what it is." I needed to get a T-shirt with that on it. It seemed to be the motto for my life.

I relaxed back into the couch. "Well, at least we can talk without being listened in on. Millicent and her dad took care of it."

"That they did." Will nodded. "They did a mighty good job of it too. I've never seen weaves like that before. They sent me the plans, but they've put a masking spell on the ones around the house."

"Doesn't that use too much power?"

"Not always. They've used a tie-off spell which minimises it, and once we have our faculties back in proper working order, we'll make it so Angelica and I share the load, which is minimal—about what it takes to make two cups of coffee."

Ah, I could totally relate to that. "Are you any closer to catching who did this or fixing our magic?"

They shared a poker-faced look. Well, that was enlightening. Not.

Will turned his upper body towards me. "We're still whittling down suspects. It's extremely hard, given the lack of evidence. We just need a breakthrough, or for them to do something that clarifies things for us. There were three thefts of personal property, and they all happened to be from families of agents. The targeted businesses were seemingly random, but for all we know, there could be a specific reason."

"Or not," Angelica said. "As Will said: it's too early to tell. We have used your photographic information, though. We've put their heights and builds into my own personal system—we don't want questions about where we received that information. I'm hoping when we get more information, we'll be able to use your talent to uncover who it is."

"I'll help whenever you need me." Trying to get away from the PIB hadn't worked so far, so I might as well save myself the energy and go with it. I did love helping people —it was more the danger I could do without. "I'm guessing you have no new news on curing us?"

Angelica sat up straighter—if that was possible. Her chin raised just a smidge. It was enough to tell me she was defensive. "We'll get there. Rome wasn't built in a day, as they say. This is a complicated matter. I assure you that you'll be one of the first to know when we have something."

I gave her a gentle smile. "It's okay. I know it's a hard task. You'll definitely get there. It's not like you to fail. I bet you've never failed at anything in your life. I have total faith in you and the PIB team."

It was meant to be encouraging, but she pressed her lips together before re-engaging her poker face. Her tone was stiff. "Thank you, Lily. Of course I'll succeed. It's what I do." She was so… Ma'am. "I take it you're available to work tomorrow if we need you?"

"Yes."

"Good. I'll call you when we need you. Now, I've got some paperwork to do, so I'll leave you young 'uns to it." She stood and walked out. Her footfalls on the stairs indicated she was going to work from her bedroom. If she'd had properly operating magic, she likely would've gone back to the PIB, but now she was homebound. At least we were safe here. Hopefully I'd sleep tonight.

Will took my hand, threading his fingers through mine. "Want to watch some TV?"

I nodded. "I've been so busy lately that I'm so far behind on *Outlander*. Can we watch that?"

He tilted his head to the side. "You just love that Jamie fellow." He smirked. "I know you."

"Well, Claire isn't bad either. I'm sure you can *suffer* through a couple of episodes."

He waggled his brows. "I'm sure I can."

I grinned and stood, pulling him up with me. At least we could enjoy tonight. Tomorrow, however, was another matter.

CHAPTER 7

The next morning, Angelica woke us at seven thirty, deciding that I was going to go into work with her and Will. Because they had to drive, and Will refused to drive the duck, we all had to go together in her car. At least the duck brought a chuckle out of me. As we left, I enquired as to why we couldn't take the duck, which elicited a dirty look from Will and a smirk from Angelica. Even though Angelica would've been game (pardon the pun), there was only going to be duck travel over Will's "dead body." We went sans quackmobile. Spoilsport.

As soon as we got in, we went to Ma'am's office. Liv, surprisingly, was there. As soon as she saw me, she grinned. "Lily! I wasn't expecting you in today." She gave me a hug.

"I wasn't expecting to be in either. Do you need help with anything?" I had to assume Ma'am had corralled her to assist, and she was going to be very busy. "I'm here just in case I'm needed out in the field." I put my bag under Ma'am's large table. My bag contained everything I might need for the day because I couldn't just magic anything to myself on short notice.

Ma'am sat in her chair, and Will sat in one of her guest chairs while Liv sat in the other. I dragged another chair from the reception area, placed it next to Liv, and sat.

Ma'am raised her hand, then opened her mouth in a little "o," likely realising she couldn't magic whatever it was to her. She picked up the phone and dialled. Crisis averted. Although I didn't think of Will's car as being a disaster, I grinned.

While Ma'am was on the phone, Liv asked, "What's so funny?"

Will shot a glare my way, but it just made me giggle. Rather than explain, I took my phone out of my bag and brought up the picture of the bright-yellow quackmobile. "That's Will's Range Rover."

Liv's mouth dropped open, and then she laughed. "Oh my, that's hilarious."

"And the horn is a quack."

"You just had to add that in, didn't you?" Will folded his arms, a surly expression on his face.

I grinned. "Of course. It's my favourite part."

"Wait till Beren sees this!" Liv's eyes glistened as she tried to stop laughing. "Can you text it to him?"

Will gave me another dirty look and turned back to Ma'am, who'd hung up. "What's on the agenda for today, Ma'am?"

Ma'am straightened her smile. "I'm waiting for some files to be brought in. Then we can go through the facts of the case so far. We just need to find one str—"

Thunder boomed and rattled the windows. Liv and I slammed our hands over our ears. It was so loud, it was as if it was coming from inside the building. Was it an earthquake? Was the building about to collapse?

Instead of another thunderclap as I expected, the buzz of magic vibrated my scalp, familiar, but I couldn't place whose it was. Sizzling echoed through Ma'am's office. Glowing blue letters fizzled like a burning sparkler into the air in front of the wall to Ma'am's left. We all stared as words formed.

At 10:00 a.m., Lloyds Bank will be £20,000,000 poorer, and there's nothing you can do about it. Do you know what PIB stands for? Pathetically Impotent Bunglers. Until next time...

The message hovered—whoever it was, was letting us take time to read it, like we were that slow. Sheesh. Fortunately, it did give me time to grab my phone and take a picture, just in case we needed it later. After about a minute, the sizzling stopped, and the letters faded. Ma'am and Will stared at each other, probably thinking about what the best response would be before they rushed into action. Ma'am's brow furrowed, and she shook her head. "We can't tell them."

Will nodded. "Agreed. We don't have enough to go on, and if it's a bluff, we'll look stupid. Even if it's legit, we don't know how they're going to do it, so there's no way to stop it happening. It's not like they can shut down every branch and all their online services. Maybe just send them a warning?"

"Hmm." She looked as if she were considering it. But then her eyes opened slightly larger. "Can you get Agent Bianchi on the phone please? Ask him to check the shields. I thought we'd redone everything."

"As far as I know, we have." Will's brow did its usual thing and wrinkled.

There was a knock at the outer door of Ma'am's office. I jumped up. "I'll get it." It was likely the documents she requested earlier. I hurried to the receptionist's office and opened the door. A short, mousy-looking woman stood there, a pile of folders in her arms. I stood aside. "Just through there." She quietly thanked me and went in.

As I stepped into Ma'am's office, Mousy was already leaving. She scurried past me and through the door, shutting it behind her. I sat in my chair. "What are you going to do?"

Ma'am drummed her fingers on the table. "Doing nothing chafes my sensibilities. I agree with you, Agent Blakesley; we need to warn Oscar. He'll deal with it discreetly."

"Who's Oscar?" Liv asked.

"He's on the bank's board of directors. He'll know who to contact to keep an eye out. This will have to be kept to witches only, for obvious reasons. If the money is taken, the normal police will be involved, and we'll let them do their thing. Maybe they'll figure out who it is before us. Our contacts inside will keep us updated. I just don't want anyone to know we've been compromised. We're already having trouble with funding. Anything else that makes us look like a bunch of hacks or has-beens, and this whole thing could get shut down."

I blinked a few times. "But that's absurd! Who would deal with witch crimes if we weren't around… I mean, you guys? It's not like witches would suddenly stop offending."

"There's politics going on that you're better off not knowing about, dear. Suffice it to say that not everyone involved in our organisation wants to see us succeed. Their interests are better served elsewhere, where they stand to gain more power. That's all I'm going to say." She looked at Liv. "Set up a meeting in the conference room for"—she looked at her watch—"ten thirty. I want Agents Bianchi, DuPree, Cardinal, Flinders, and Johanssen."

Liv stood. "Consider it done. I've got everything I need in Agent Bianchi's office. Do you require anything else?"

"Just that, at the moment. Actually, now that I can't use my magic, I'd like you to attend the meeting too, to take notes." Ma'am turned her gaze on me. "Lily, you can go through these files. There are printouts of all the criminals we've incarcerated over the last ten years who are still in prison. Read through them and pick out all the ones who have threatened the PIB. For all we know, someone *inside* is pulling the strings."

Will nodded. "From the correspondence so far, it sounds personal, as if whoever it is holds a grudge."

"I couldn't pinpoint it exactly, but the magic felt familiar. Kind of like when you see someone and you're sure you know them but not from where."

Ma'am's brows drew down. "Are you sure you can't place it? Think, Lily. This is very important." As if I didn't know how important it was. I forced my eyes to stare forward rather than go for a roll.

"It might be just a case of I've felt magic like it before, but it's not the exact magic. I don't know. If I figure it out, I'll tell you. Also, are you sure whoever's doing this is not just doing that to mess with you? I mean, disabling your power is an awesome ploy so they can commit crimes without worrying about the PIB showing up. Stealing twenty million pounds sounds like a wonderful end game to me, and a great red herring." I was just putting it out there because sometimes it *was* just about the money.

Ma'am looked down her nose at me, gravity in her gaze. "True… but in my experience, nothing is ever that simple. We'll keep our minds open, and we need to look at every angle. The stones we leave unturned today have the ability to become the mountain in our way tomorrow." Wow, that was profound. And that's why she was Ma'am. She stood. "Okay, Agent Blakesley. Let's go."

Will stood and looked down at me. "I'll see you later. Do not leave this building. I'll text you later, but you're coming home with us."

I smiled. "Of course. Have fun." He gave me a "yeah right" look; then he, Liv, and Ma'am left. I stared at the pile of files on the desk, took a deep breath, and sighed. Looked like I had a mountain to climb myself. If only I had a pet squirrel to keep me company. Lamenting my lack of squirrel companionship, I grabbed the first file and got to work.

A couple of hours later, Ma'am returned, Liv on her heels carrying a notebook. Tension flowed into the room with them. A few grey hairs had escaped Ma'am's bun, and her harried expression told a tale of a woman under pressure. I imagined her days were stressful but add a lack of magic to speed things up, and the poker face was too hard to maintain. "Is everything all right?" I asked. "Would you like me to fetch you a cup of tea?"

She pulled her chair out a tad too firmly, and it hit the wall behind it. Ma'am pressed her lips together and plonked down before pulling herself closer to the table. She looked at me. "That would be lovely. Thank you, dear."

Liv sat next to me, and I turned to her. "Do you want anything while I'm down there?"

"Yes, thanks. Tea and scones. Is that okay?"

"Of course it is. I'll be back soon." I hurried downstairs, eager to return so I could find out what had happened to cause Ma'am to lose it. Okay, so it's not a normal person's version of losing it, but she hardly ever got ruffled, and this was her being super ruffled.

I finished ordering our food and found a spot at a vacant table to wait. They weren't delivering to offices because their magic was on the fritz, and there weren't enough staff to deliver by hand. The curse was affecting the most mundane things. Across the cafeteria, a forty-something-year-old male agent was tucking into a meal. He stood out because he had a fluorescent-pink mohawk. Someone must have accidentally used magic to do their hair this morning. I grinned. He probably hadn't had time to fix it, and I doubted he dared use his magic. But who could blame him for forgetting? For all these witches, using magic would be second nature, just part of their day.

"Hey, stranger." Beren pulled out the chair next to me and sat.

"Hey, yourself. What's happening?" His smile fell. "That great, huh?"

"Pretty much. Are you here grabbing food?"

Hmm, he obviously didn't want to talk about it, or likely couldn't. "Waiting for my order, then taking it up to Ma'am and Liv. That meeting must've been a doozy."

He made a motion of zipping his lips. "I'm not saying anything. You'll have to hear it from the horse's mouth."

"Ooh, if she heard you called her a horse...." I laughed.

He cocked his head to the side. "You know I didn't mean it like that."

"Scared, are we?"

"I still can't tell you."

"Damn. You cluey agent, you."

One of the cafeteria staff came to my table, a large tray filled with my order in his hands. "Here you go. If you could bring the tray back later, that would be great."

"Not a problem. Thanks." I stood and looked at B. "Well, since you won't spill the beans, I'm leaving."

"I knew you only wanted me for my information." He pouted as if he were upset.

"You know it." I grinned. "Enjoy your lunch. Have you got much on this arvo?"

"Loads. Can you tell Liv that I'll be back to take her home at around six?"

"Will do." I picked the tray up. "Bye."

"Bye."

Whatever had happened must be monumental. Normally Beren would give me at least a hint, unless it was something top secret. But he shut it down at record pace, and he didn't look like budging at all. Had the money been taken? Maybe that's what the emergency was. But why get so upset after the fact when they knew it was going to happen? And it would be like Ma'am said: they'd just get the police to deal with it for the time being. Surely things would get back to normal soon.

When I returned, the door was shut, and I needed both hands, so I knocked with my forehead. Gus happened to be wandering past. "Hello, Miss Lily. Using your head, I see." He chuckled. "Would you like some help?"

"Oh, hey, Gus. That would be great, thanks." But just before he could open the door, Liv answered it.

"Looks like someone beat me to it." He gave Liv a nod. "Hello, Miss Olivia."

"Hi, Gus." Her brow furrowed as she looked from Gus, to me, to Gus.

"He was about to open the door for me, but you beat him to it."

"Ah, I see." She stepped aside. As I walked through to Ma'am's office, Liv said, "So, how's the family?" I walked faster. There was no way I wanted to hear any of Gus's stories right before eating.

I placed the tray on the table and gave Ma'am her tea and shortbread. "I got some biscuits for you. I know you didn't ask for any, but I figured you might be hungry."

"Thank you, dear." She brought the cup to her lips, shut her eyes, and took a sip. "Ahh, I needed that."

I took the other stuff off the tray and put the tray on the floor, then tucked into my coffee, and my cheese-and-tomato toasted sandwich. Liv's conversation with Gus over, she'd shut the door, and was pulling her chair out to sit. Now that she was here for support—just in case Ma'am got irritated with me—I could ask about what was going on. "Um… what happened at the meeting? You don't look very happy." I sat lower in my chair, anticipating an annoyed brush-off.

She carefully placed her teacup on the saucer. "I can't say much because I can't"—she waved a hand in the air to indicate the lack of a bubble of silence—"but let's just say that we're being blamed for some money going missing and leave it at that, shall we?" She smoothed her hair back from her forehead.

Liv gave me a grim nod. "How'd you go with that lot?" She tipped her head towards the folders strewn across the desk.

"Yes, dear, and could you have been a bit neater about it?"

Yes, I was messy, but I couldn't be perfect… and that comment was totally tongue-in-cheek. "You know it's all part of my charm." I grinned. Hmm, I didn't think I'd ever seen Ma'am look so unimpressed. I hurried on. "The mess is part of my order. It would probably be easier if I had a whiteboard or something where I could pin the profiles and draw lines between them, like they do on TV crime shows." The files on the desk had a paper clip attaching a mugshot of the criminal plus a brief rundown of their crime, time in jail, threat, date/s of threat/s made, and level of power, both magical and in terms of support on the outside. "I've arranged them from most likely to be a problem to least likely, but some of them have connections to each other, either after meeting inside or they knew each other before going to jail."

"Thank you, dear. That's very helpful. I'll go through these with James later." She picked up her phone and asked someone to come and fit a large whiteboard to her wall. It was nice to be taken seriously for a change. As soon as she hung up, her phone rang. Her voice, when she answered, was *accommodating*. I'd never heard her be so friendly. Unease breathed creepily down my nape, raising the hairs. "Yes, sir. Of course. Immediately." She hung up, shut her eyes for a moment, then opened them, and stood. This couldn't be good.

"Is everything okay?" I figured she'd say yes because she wasn't one to spill her worries on others, but you never knew.

She ran a hand down her tie, smoothing it against her shirt. "Of course. I'll be back later. And, Olivia, you have work to do. Maybe get Lily to help you." Without waiting for an answer, she strode out.

Liv and I looked at each other. I bit my lip. "That doesn't seem good."

"No, it doesn't. And before you ask, I don't know what it's about, but I can guess."

I waited for a moment, but Liv didn't continue. "You can't hint and then leave me hanging. What's your guess?"

"I can't say."

"What the hell?" I was about to say more, but she held up her hand in a stop gesture.

As she spoke, she sat at Ma'am's desk, opened her notebook, and wrote. "Sorry. I shouldn't have said anything. Anyway, we need to work on the stuff Ma'am gave me before." She turned the note she'd written around so I could read it.

The PIB big bosses will probably have heard about the money. Oh, crap. They weren't exactly supportive, from what I'd heard. Was it because they didn't like Ma'am, and they didn't have anyone else to fill her shoes at the moment? Or were they frustrated at their lack of government funding? I wasn't even sure how that all worked. Maybe the PIB was privately funded?

"I'd love to help. I'm stuck here all day, so I might as well."

Liv quietly closed the notebook and stood. "Let's go to Mill's office."

As we travelled along the corridor, I wondered if we'd ever be able to trust anyone who wasn't part of our group. "Liv, why does everything have to be so hard?"

She sighed. "I wish I knew, Lily. I wish I knew."

CHAPTER 8

While Angelica, Will, and James bumbled along without proper magic and tried to deal with the fallout from the bank theft, the day had arrived for me to visit Millicent's dad. Because I wasn't supposed to go anywhere by myself, Imani drove me to Millicent and James's place. We didn't know how tired her dad would be after mucking around with my tattoo, so we thought it best to just drive.

Millicent answered the door, the baby in her arms. When we were inside, I gave her a hug. "Can I hold my niece, pretty please?"

"You sure can." She happily handed her over, and I cradled her to me, getting a good sniff of her baldish head. Babies, when they were clean, had the sweetest smell. Once I'd cooed over her for a few minutes, Millicent's dad arrived via the reception room. After Millicent let him in, I reluctantly handed my niece to Imani, who was also eager for a cuddle.

Her dad smiled reassuringly. "We'll do this in the living room, where it's more comfortable."

My stomach fluttered with nerves. If this worked, I'd be overjoyed, but if it didn't…. I'd had enough experience with disappointment that I'd be fine either way, eventually. I sat on the couch, my "bad" arm next to him. "Do you think the curse will interfere with what you're going to do?"

"No. It's only a problem if you cast a spell, but I won't be asking you to do that."

Millicent gave me a gentle smile. "He's really good at what he does, Lily. Don't worry; you're in the best of hands. Now I'll leave you to it. If you need anything, Imani and I will be in the kitchen."

"Thanks." I sat on the edge of the couch and tapped my foot on the ground.

"Relax, Lily. The first part won't hurt, and if I'm going to do anything that might surprise you, I'll let you know beforehand, and you can say yay or nay. Okay?"

I giggled at the rhyme. Ordinarily, I might be able to hide that, but being nervous put a serious chink in my self-control. "Um, okay." I didn't really have a choice.

He chuckled. "You can sit back. That's what I meant by relax. You're making me nervous." Gah, I didn't want that. I wanted things to go as smoothly as possible.

I settled back and held out my arm. He took it in gentle but firm fingers. "I'm going to start by having another look at things. You'll feel a bit of warmth, but that's all." As he got to work, I stared at the blank TV screen on the wall opposite. The TV was bookended by white shelves filled with, you guessed it, books. I wasn't sure how long this was going to take, but if it was a while, maybe I should've grabbed one of those first.

After about ten minutes, he released my arm, and the subtle warmth of his magic dissipated. His face, like others before him when they looked at me, was carefully devoid of expression. Great. Not. "Is it bad news?"

"Not exactly. I know how to disable the tracking spell. But it's booby-trapped. I know the spell, so I can take measures to avoid the repercussions, but it still poses some danger. Whoever did this definitely has an army background."

"That's actually a positive. Well, not positive about the army background, but maybe we can figure out who did this now that we have extra information."

"True, but it also means you're not dealing with an amateur. Anyway, I'm sure we can save that discussion for another time. Right now, I'm going to attempt to remove the spell. It could take a while, and the heat might become almost unbearable. Do you still want me to try?"

"Yes." There was no hesitation in my answer. Maybe if we could disable the tracking part of the tattoo, the other spells would be easier to get rid of too. I just wanted the damn tattoo gone. I scowled at it. "Do we need a safe word for if it gets too much?"

His forehead creased. "No. Once I start pulling the threads apart, I can't stop. If I break my magic connection,

I'll set off the booby trap. What the result will be, I can't say, but we could both end up dead. Once you're in, Lily, you're in, no matter how painful it becomes."

Oh, crap. Did I still want to do this? I swallowed. Yes, yes I did. I wouldn't let the snake group have any more power over me than I could help. For that, I could suffer for an afternoon. Whatever pain I went through would be a small price to pay—it was only one afternoon after all. I met Robert's enquiring gaze. "Yes, I'd like to go ahead. Don't worry if I cry or scream or whatever. I'll try not to make any noise, but if I can't help it, I'll just have to let it out, but I can cope. Just don't stop."

He gave a curt nod. "Understood."

My heart ratcheted up a notch as he took my wrist again, and his magic unfurled over my scalp, neck, and down my arm. Robert's familiar magic wasn't painful at first. Five minutes passed. Maybe I could do this without any dramas. What a lovely change.

While he worked, I glanced from his hand on the tattoo to his face and around the room. I wanted to know how he thought it was going, but I dared not break his concentration, and I didn't want to stare at him the whole time because he'd think I was a weirdo.

I estimated another five minutes had passed. Feeling quite smug that this was going more easily than I'd thought, I settled further into the couch, and the tension in my jaw went away.

And that's when it hit.

The motherload of all pain.

I had just enough time to take in Robert scrunching his eyes shut and gritting his teeth before scalding heat ripped through my arm. It was as if my arm was on fire and my wrist was melting. I screamed and shut my eyes. It was all I could do not to rip my arm out of his hold. I knew I was crying, but I couldn't stop it, and all I could feel was burning. I leaned away, did my best not to go too far, but it was unbearable. Robert grunted, likely his way of reminding me what might happen if I disengaged.

And still, my arm was being seared from the inside out.

I hadn't thought it possible to hate RP any more than I already did, but it was, indeed, possible. If it wasn't for them, I wouldn't be living through hell right now.

I sobbed and groaned, and I didn't even care who heard. My eyes were still closed—not that it did much, but it was easier to retreat into myself, and it helped conserve a tiny bit of energy. Maybe that minuscule amount of energy would be what got me over the line.

Time lost meaning as I endured the searing barrage.

At some point, Robert's whispered chants broke through. My shallow breathing rasped loudly. Stabbing pain lanced my stomach, even more excruciating than the all-encompassing fire. Dizziness swirled. Was I about to pass out?

And then it was done. Robert released my wrist, and the pain was gone, leaving me tender and raw. I was so afraid to move, in case it came back, that I kept my eyes closed.

"Lily, can you hear me? It's done. You can open your eyes." Exhaustion dripped from his words.

I braced myself and did as he asked.

Wow, the pain really was gone, and boy did Millicent's dad look like he hadn't slept for two weeks while simultaneously wrestling crocodiles. Millicent and Imani stood in the middle of the room, staring at us, their gazes expectant.

"Did it work?" My voice came out in an unintentional whisper.

He smiled. "I'm pleased to announce that it was a resounding success."

"Thank you so, so, so, so, so much!" Joy skipped through me. I surprised myself by giving him a hug. "You're incredible." I released him and sat back, my cheeks heating. The English weren't known for their spontaneous and enthusiastic displays of affection. And I wasn't normally like that, so I hoped he hadn't been too put out.

He laughed. "It's fine, Lily. I've risked my life for far less worthy causes than yours before. I have a feeling that whoever did this is a threat we want neutralised as quickly as possible. So now you'll be free to roam without being tracked. The other two spells aren't clear to me yet, but we'll set another session for next week, if that's okay. I'm not as young as I used to be. I think I could sleep until then and not stir."

Millicent bent and gave her dad a hug. "I'll get you some tea, coffee, and sandwiches. That was a real marathon." She turned and left, while Imani sat next to me.

"How long did that take?" I asked her.

"A tad over three hours, love. And the screams." She grimaced. "I wanted to come in and stop it, but Mill forbade me. You really know how to take it, Lily. I knew you were tough, but...."

My heart wriggled with happiness at the compliment, weird as that compliment was. "It was the most painful experience I've ever been through. Can't say I'm in a hurry to do it again."

Robert raised his brows. "But, Lily, if you want to disable the other spells, you'll have to. You may not have a choice."

"Can I be knocked out for it? Like under general anaesthetic?"

He rubbed his chin. "I'm not sure. It might be possible, but it would make it a riskier proposition. I'll think about it and consult with Beren. He's a clever lad, especially when it comes to medicine. I'll get back to you."

He was right: there was no way I could avoid it. We needed to banish the RP spells from my system. We didn't even know what they could do. A little burst of happiness filled me at the thought they were livid at being thwarted now they could no longer track my movements. It was definitely worth the suffering. "Thanks. I appreciate it." I glared at the stupid tattoo. Oh, hang on a minute. I squinted, although why people squinted to see better was beyond me. I could see less of what I was looking at when I did that, not more. I held my wrist in front of Imani. "Tell me I'm not imagining things."

She held my arm steady while she perused the tattoo. She gasped. "You're not imagining anything. The tail *has* disappeared!" She stared at Robert. "You sure have some strong magic. Impressive. Ma'am could use someone like you at the PIB."

He smiled. "I'm afraid I plan on staying retired. I'll help family when they need it, but I've spent too many years coming and going, and now I just want to spend time with my loved ones. Millicent's mother and I have a holiday planned for spring. We're off to Spain."

"That sounds lovely," I said. "I wish I could go to Spain."

Millicent came in. "Food's ready. Let's adjourn to the family room."

Although I was tired, a small amount of marzipan had been removed from the huge container I'd been lugging around. That was one more horrific piece I didn't have to eat, so my load felt lighter. The problem was, sometimes there were worse things than marzipan. I just hoped the universe wouldn't send them my way.

CHAPTER 9

The next day, I tagged along to headquarters with Ma'am and Will. Unfortunately, we didn't take the quackmobile—it might have gone some way to making the journey more cheerful. In the afternoon, I was supposed to visit two crime scenes with them and take photos in a bid to uncover more clues.

Ma'am hardly said a word the whole way into work, and once I was safely ensconced in Millicent's office, Ma'am and Will had hurried off to meetings. So I was more than a little surprised as I bit into my chocolate cake—from the cafeteria —when only thirty minutes after they left, Will blew into the room like a hungry dog who'd just heard the rustle of a chip packet.

I halted, the fork halfway to my mouth. Liv looked up from her computer. "Did you forget something?"

"Lily, we need your help pronto. You brought your camera today, didn't you?"

"Of course I did. You told me I'd need it." Men. "What's up?"

"I'll tell you in the car. We have to get going." He ran a hand through his hair, his body half turned to leave.

"Right. Okay." I stood, put my coat on, and grabbed my camera from my bag. "See ya, Liv. I guess I'll be back later." Whatever was going on must be major—as much as Will was known for his cranky demeanour, I'd hardly ever seen him agitated.

"Bye, guys. Stay safe."

We didn't talk on the jog to the car. Will was preoccupied with whatever was going on, and I could be patient and wait till we got in the car to ask questions… believe it or not. In the basement car park, Will led me to a black BMW SUV. Such an obvious spy car, but black was a cool colour, or non-colour for those fanatics who had to say black and white weren't colours whenever an unsuspecting person called them such.

He opened the back door for me, and I climbed in. Will went around and got into the back seat via the other side. Ma'am sat in the front passenger seat, and an agent I'd never met before was driving. Ma'am turned to look at me. "Lily, I'd like you to meet Agent Lyon."

The guy gave me a wave without turning. He met my gaze in the rear-view mirror. He looked to be mid-thirties and had a mane of dirty blond hair framing a handsome face and blue eyes. When he smiled, a fair few wrinkles decorated the corners of his eyes. "Pleased to meet you, Lily."

"Likewise." I clicked my belt buckle in.

"Agent Lyon is accompanying us because he still has fully functioning magic—he was on leave when *things* happened." The distaste in her voice at "things" was palpable and appropriate. My room was starting to resemble a war zone—tidying the normal way was not high on my list of skills or things I liked to do. Will had warned me this morning that if I couldn't keep my stuff in order, he'd move back to his place… alone. Despite that horrible prospect, I still hadn't managed to put stuff away. Maybe I'd do it tonight….

"Where are we going, and why?" Maybe someone would finally answer my questions. "Is there a BOS?"

"*Excuse me*, Lily!" Ma'am's head whiplashed around, her eyes wide. "We don't speak like that, thank you."

Huh? My heart hammered. What had I done? Will smirked and jumped to my defence. "She said B not P." Even Agent Lyon let out a low chuckle.

Ma'am turned around calmly, as if nothing had happened. "Carry on, then."

"Um, a bubble of silence. Are we protected by one?" I would definitely have to mind my Bs and Qs next time. I laughed internally at my bad joke.

"Yes, dear. Agent Lyon is a professional."

We drove out into a crisp, sunny day, Agent Lyon turning right onto the street, then accelerating to a speed that I was sure had to be over the limit. He must have had a no-notice spell on the BMW. "So, where are we going?"

Ma'am answered, "The National Gallery."

Will looked at me, concern etched into his forehead. I knew what he was asking. "Yes. I'll be fine." He gave a quick nod. I wasn't sure how much, if anything, they'd told Agent Lyon about my special talent, but seeing as how it was meant to be secret, and we didn't know who to trust, I was hoping he had no idea. Who knew what excuse they'd given him for me being here. Although Ma'am may have said nothing in her usual "I'm the boss; I don't have to explain myself" way.

"And why? I don't imagine you've decided you want to admire some artworks today."

"You would be correct, dear. The person who sent the threat about the bank heist has just sent another threat—they're targeting artworks at the gallery."

I wrinkled my brow. "But that's silly. Wouldn't those pictures be so famous that they'd be impossible to sell?" How would you explain away a Canaletto everyone knew was supposed to be hanging in the National Gallery?

Will shook his head. "You'd be surprised. Some rich, very private people wouldn't care. In fact, they'd see it as a coup and take great pleasure in buying and hanging something the whole world was looking for. They have ultimate control over who sees the painting. I would think the sellers would be targeting rich crime moguls."

"And has the crime already happened?" Last time they'd

given us a warning, and there was no reason we had to speed to get there after the fact.

"No." Will looked at his phone. "We have fifteen minutes."

"Um, I know I haven't lived here very long, but isn't it impossible for us to get to central London in that time?" Unless Agent Lyon had special powers to slow time, there was no way we'd make it.

"I've sent three of our able-magicked agents there. They arrived the usual way. They're holding down the fort till we arrive. They'll hopefully be able to thwart any efforts to steal anything."

My eyes widened. "But what if it's a ploy to disable the few uncursed agents you have?" How could they not think of this?

"It might very well be, dear, but we're ahead of them there. When this first happened, we didn't want it happening again, so we've inoculated, for want of a better word, all our unaffected agents."

"Oh, that's good." At least they'd been able to do that much. Right now, the world was these witches' oyster because so many agents were on the fritz. Imagine what would happen if all witchy criminals in the UK knew they had free rein.

As we drove, Ma'am received a couple of phone calls. The second one came through as we sat in London traffic about one mile from our destination. "Good. Okay. We'll be there soon. Stay vigilant, and good job." She hung up and turned to Agent

Lyon. "They've thwarted the theft. As soon as they sensed magic, they threw up a shield. It worked, but I don't know how much energy they have left. If they throw another major attack our way, we could still be in for a negative outcome. Maybe you should travel there, and I'll take over driving."

"Yes, Ma'am." He put the car in park—we were stopped at lights, and even if they went green, we'd be at a crawl—and vanished. Ma'am awkwardly climbed over to the driver's seat.

"But aren't we in more danger now we have no protection?" I didn't want to state the obvious, but maybe it wasn't so obvious to Ma'am, who thought she was invincible.

"Yes, dear, and our *BOS* spell is gone too. So, less talk."

Right. Ma'am didn't always answer, but when she did, it was direct. I couldn't fault her for that. I'd rather know where I stood. "Okay." I chewed my fingernail as we crawled to Trafalgar Square. What if they launched another attack? Would they try and kill the agents? I hoped they wouldn't steal any art, but surely the agents' lives were more important.

"They are, dear, but if we fail at this, we'll also be in the gallery's bad books." Damn mind-reading talent. "Yes, I know." She smiled. I sighed dramatically. "It's worth the risk."

I agree. Why talk when I didn't have to?

"Just so you know, if we're in a crowded room, I may not be able to pick up on your thoughts, so talk to me."

Okay. I grinned. I liked being a smarty pants.

It took another ten minutes to get to the gallery. Ma'am

parked against the double yellow lines. I guessed she couldn't care less if we got a ticket. The PIB could afford it, even with their supposedly dismal budget. As we got out of the car, Will came and stood next to me and said, "Stay close to me at all times." I nodded. I hadn't planned on being a hero today, and all I had to protect myself with was faulty magic—he at least had a gun.

We hurried past the long line outside. Had the gallery workers given patrons some excuse to send them outside, or had the witches cast a spell? None of us were using a no-notice spell, so everyone stared at the three black-suit clad, official-looking people. I'd worn my suit to work today because I knew we were going out in the field. I just hadn't expected it to be here and so early in the day.

The staff ushered us through to the spectacular main foyer. If I hadn't been here before, my mouth would have dropped open at the colourful, detailed ceilings and mosaic-tiled floors. As soon as we were inside, Agent Lyon met us. "Can I have a word?" he asked Ma'am.

She gave a nod, and they moved up the stairs, away from everyone. Heads close together, they spoke. My neck sore with tension, I glanced around—we were worried about magic, but what if someone attacked us the normal way? It always paid to pay attention. In the high-ceilinged space, I felt like a mouse out in the open with hawks flying overhead. I edged closer to Will until our arms were almost touching. There was safety in numbers... at least that's what I told myself.

Ma'am and Agent Lyon finished their conversation. He

walked further into the gallery, and Ma'am motioned for us to join her. We took the stairs two at a time. She spoke with a quiet voice. "The agents have pinpointed the paintings that were targeted—they would've had to choose them with magic one by one, maybe with a spell that would anchor them to the major spell that would've pulled them out of the gallery. There was also a significant amount of power thrown at the place, so unless they have a large pool of witches, they shouldn't be able to repeat that today. I'll be stationing agents here for the next couple of days, at least. I'll show you both the paintings they tried to steal." She winked at me, which I understood to mean she'd like me to take photos and see if we could find any other clues.

Our footsteps clacked on the hard floor and echoed through the space. Self-conscious, I tried to walk more quietly, but it was a big ask. These were unforgiving floors. I needed those silent-as-a-ninja nurse shoes. You would think spies would use them too. Seemed there was a huge market for those things. Maybe I should go into business. Setting up an online store couldn't be that hard.

"Lily, what are you going on about?" Ma'am raised one eyebrow. "Is it really like that in your head the whole time?"

My cheeks heated. I shrugged. "I find it entertaining. I guess you can't please everyone, and considering I'm in my own head, I shouldn't have to try."

"Well, I can't very well block anything at the moment, but as soon as I can, I'll guarantee you that I will."

I tilted my head to the side. "Gee, thanks."

Ma'am stopped in front of a painting titled *The Ambas-*

sadors by Hans Holbein. Two shifty-eyed, bearded young men stood facing the audience, a table filled with a plethora of things between them. She gave a slow, firm nod. I took the lens cap off my Nikon and called upon my talent as I pointed the camera at the picture. *Show me who cast the spell to steal this artwork.*

A man appeared, facing the painting. His bulky coat hid his frame, but it was the same coat I'd seen on the man in the bedroom at the agent's house. I wandered around so I could see his face. He wasn't in the position to hide everything with a balaclava in such a public place, but his Fedora was pulled low, and his bushy moustache and beard covered his mouth and chin. Shoulder-length orange hair descended from underneath the hat. He likely wore a wig and fake facial hair. I snapped a few shots anyway—hopefully his nose was his real one, and we could at least ferret that information away. The next step would be to get hold of the security video so we could see which entrance he'd used and follow his movements throughout the gallery.

I stepped back from the painting and took one more picture. I lowered the camera. "Will, can you stand in front of the painting? And stand up straight." He did as I asked. I directed him to exactly where the other guy had stood. Then I took a couple of normal shots of Will for a height comparison. "Great. Thanks." I turned to Ma'am. "So, where's the next one?"

"Right this way."

We spent the next thirty minutes on edge, waiting for another attack, but we managed to get the job done with no further incidents, at which point, Agent Lyon drove us back to headquarters.

Second crisis averted. Thank goodness. From what I gathered, Ma'am was already on notice because of the bank job. Another unhappy organisation was not what the PIB needed, especially a government one. In fact, I'd say this had been a success—PIB agents had actually prevented a crime. But would we be so lucky next time?

Agent Lyon returned out into the field, so it was only Ma'am, Will, and me in her office. She'd called James, who was on his way from another part of the building. While we waited for him, Ma'am and Will peered at my camera screen, studying the photos I'd taken. They couldn't put them on Ma'am's laptop, in case someone saw them and wondered how and why. Not that anyone knew who the subject of the photos was, but if it ever came out, we'd be leaving ourselves open to the discovery of my talent by the wider witch world. Any secrets we kept would work to our advantage.

Will sat back, and Ma'am looked up from the camera. She handed it to me. "Well done, Lily. It's not conclusive, but we have a small amount of new information, and at this stage, I'll take wh—"

Sizzling filled the office. Ma'am and I gave each other a quick look of surprise before the message wrote itself against her wall. I flicked my camera to video mode and filmed as glowing blue words formed.

Well played, Agent DuPree. Well played. I suppose one can get lucky once. Maybe I made things too easy for you. Next time, I won't underestimate your skill. But I don't want this game to end too soon, so I suppose I'll have to keep you in it a while longer. Toodle-oo.

James walked in, halting as soon as he saw the words. But he didn't get long to look, as they faded away. Ma'am slammed her hand on the table, and we all jumped. "Damn our incompetence! How in heavens is this magic getting past our new shields." She turned an angry glare on my brother.

He didn't bat an eye. He'd always been calm under pressure, and so was Ma'am—usually—but today things must be getting to her. What the hell had been said in that meeting with her superiors? James sat down and placed his hands in his lap. "No one has breached our shields. If they had, our alarm would have sounded. I would posit that it's coming from inside the building."

Not one to waste time with apologies, her poker face reasserted itself. "You're probably right, Agent Bianchi. Right. Now we need to weed the person out. But how…?" That was going to be tricky. Where would they start? I mean, Ma'am could read minds, but it was obviously an able-bodied agent, or it wouldn't have worked properly, so she couldn't just pick up an errant thought from them, and I doubted questioning would get them to admit they were involved. Ma'am stood. "I'll be back in five. In the meantime, I suggest you go through Lily's photos." Her stately pace as she left the room and shut the door belied the turmoil I imagined was wreaking havoc inside her mind. What a disaster.

"I guess you need this." I handed James my camera.

"Thanks."

While Ma'am was out, I felt freer to ask questions. She had enough to contend with, and I didn't want to add to her stress. "Are we any closer to finding a cure for the curse?"

Will folded his arms. "Not that I know of. Beren's working with Dr Finnegan. But because B can't perform magic, he has to instruct the good doctor on what to do. It's going very slowly, apparently. B's excellent at what he does —not everyone can keep up with him."

"Mill's dad is also what I'd class as excellent. He got rid of RP's tracking, as you know."

Will smiled. "And we owe him for that. I was thinking a top-shelf bottle of booze."

"He doesn't drink." James didn't bother looking up from the photos as he answered.

"What do you think he'd like?" I asked.

James shrugged. "I have no idea. Maybe ask Mill." He turned the camera off and handed it to me. "You know… maybe I should ask him to help Beren. But we won't tell anyone, just so we don't ruffle any feathers."

My mouth dropped open. "You'd go behind Ma'am's back." I thought I knew my brother, but maybe I didn't.

He rolled his eyes. "Of course not, dopey. As if I'd do anything behind her back."

The door opened, and Ma'am entered. "Do what behind whose back?" Trust her to return at just the right moment. I suppressed a smile.

James relayed our conversation. Ma'am sat and drummed her fingers on the desk, likely thinking it through. When she met James's gaze, her lips were quirked up in a cat who'd eaten the canary smile. Poor canary. I frowned. Ma'am shifted her eyes my way, then rolled them. Being on guard and controlling my thoughts all the time was not going well. I supposed I should just give up at this point. She shook her head and focussed on James again.

"I think that's a wonderful idea. He did well with the house spells, and he's helped Lily. Can you set up a meeting with him tonight at your place?"

"I'll see. I know he was wiped out after Lily's thing."

Ma'am waved her hand. "Whenever he's ready is fine, but the sooner, the better, obviously. Now, I'd like to move onto other things. We'll finish this conversation tonight." Her meaningful eyebrow raise conveyed that we weren't safe to talk about things here, which made sense if someone from inside the PIB was sabotaging us. Again. Man, the world was full of horrible people. Life would be so much easier if everyone was decent and nice. "Right, I have work to get through. Agent Bianchi, you can stay here. Will, you can help Imani with something she's working on—she's in her office. And, Lily, you can help Olivia with whatever she's doing. We might postpone that investigative appointment you were going to attend. I'll see you back here at six."

"Yes, Ma'am," Will and I both answered. Will and I kissed goodbye out in the hall, and I made my way to Millicent's office. Unfortunately, Liv wasn't there, and her phone was on top of her closed laptop. I waited for five minutes, then decided to have a wander around, see if I could find her. Maybe she'd gone to get food.

I ambled down to the cafeteria. It was half full, but none

of the occupants was Liv. Had she merely gone to the bathroom? Knowing my luck, I'd just missed her, and she was already back in her office. I was about to turn and leave when my nostrils caught the tempting fragrance of coffee. Since I was already here, I might as well grab some, and maybe a chocolate muffin. I smiled. My brain had the best ideas sometimes. I ordered coffee, tea for Liv, and two chocolate muffins—no one could say I neglected my friends.

Food and beverage in hand, I made my way back to Millicent and Liv's office. As I passed Beren's office, the door swung open, and someone stepped out in front of me. I almost managed to dodge, but it happened so quickly, we collided. My hands, which each held one coffee and a bag with a muffin, pushed back into my chest. To compensate, I jumped back, but a squirt of coffee still shot out of the small drinking hole and onto my white shirt. Damn.

"Oh, heavens. I'm so sorry, Lily." Dr Finnegan stood there, eyes wide, a hand on either side of his head, his hair poking out messily around his fingers. Dark bags puffed the skin beneath his eyes. Someone was working way too hard.

"That's okay. I'm sure it'll wash clean, and not too much was spilled, so it's fine."

He nodded. "Okay, okay. As long as you're not burnt?"

"No. I'm fine."

"Okay, good." He turned and hurried down the hallway. Whatever he was racing to must be urgent.

Beren appeared at his open office door—Dr Finnegan had forgotten to close it. Normally relaxed, Beren's forehead wrinkled. "Oh, it's you. What just happened?"

I shrugged. "Dr Finnegan was hurrying out of your office, and he crashed into me. Not a big deal. He seems a bit overworked."

Beren glanced down the hallway as the frazzled doctor disappeared around a corner. "He's not any more over-worked than the rest of us. We haven't even done anything today. That's why he was here—he's not feeling well, and he's going home early. He's not sure if he's in tomorrow either." He pressed his lips together. "This damn curse is never going to be lifted at this rate. I'm just worried it's still infecting people. We thought we had stopped it from hurting anyone else, but Dr Finnegan is having the same symptoms the rest of us did, and the nurse that works with him also went home unwell this morning." He rubbed his temples.

I sucked in a breath. "That's not good. Do you think it's contagious? We can't afford to lose more agents. Does Ma'am know?"

"I'm going to call her now. I have no idea if it's contagious, but if it is, we're sunk until we find a cure. How are we supposed to beat this thing?"

I lowered my voice. "Ma'am's working on something, but I can't say here because, well, you know." I looked each way and up at the ceiling. "But would they really make it contagious? Can you imagine what would happen if every witch caught it?" Although, you would think the ones who started the curse would know how to stop it, and they could make a lot of money curing people, but that would also leave them exposed—it would be way too easy to figure out who it was if they did that.

Beren gave me a worried look, then his expression cleared, and he glanced at my hands. "So, you're extra hungry today?"

Apparently it was time to change the subject. I grinned. "Come on, B. Don't be silly. This is normal for me. You know that."

"Oh, my mistake." He smiled. "You wouldn't happen to be going to see the most gorgeous woman at headquarters, would you?"

"But I'm standing right here." I snorted. "Yes, I'm off to see Liv. She wasn't there before, but I'm hoping she's back. This food isn't going to eat itself, although I'm sure I could eat both muffins if I had to."

"I bet you could. Anyway, say hello to her for me. Tell her, I'll be at her office at five thirty."

"Will do."

"Oh, and congrats." He grinned. "I heard about what happened at your brother's place."

He must be talking about my tracking spell being deactivated. Happiness warmed my insides. "Thanks. One down, two to go. Anyway, I'd better leave you to it. See you later."

"Later." He shut his door, and I returned to Mill's office. This time, Liv was there. She had, indeed, been in the bathroom.

"What the hell happened to you, clumsy klutz?"

I looked down at my coffee-stained shirt. "Small accident. Dr Finnegan walked into me. It wasn't actually my fault." I stuck my tongue out.

She laughed. Miracles will never cease. She eyed the

food. "I see you've brought supplies." She indicated the food and tea.

"Yep. I look after my friends, even if they insult my ableness." I placed everything on the table and grabbed a muffin. I wanted to talk about the curse, but it wasn't safe. Maybe I could make a bubble of silence. I mean, what could go wrong? Okay, so plenty could go wrong. Boy, this was frustrating. Stupid curse. I couldn't even whisk us away to Ma'am's place where everything was eavesdropping proofed. "So, is there any work I can help you with? I'm stuck here all afternoon again, and it's going to be extremely boring if I have nothing to do." I bit into my muffin.

"I've got loads of stuff you can help with." She stood and grabbed a pile of files sitting on Millicent's desk. She handed them to me, then her phone rang. "Hello, Olivia speaking." She listened for a moment while I placed the files on Liv's desk in front of me. "Yes. Coming now." She hung up and looked at me. "We've been summoned to Ma'am's favourite conference room."

I placed my muffin on the desk and frowned. It would have to wait. "Oh, okay." It was a surprise but not a shock. When at HQ anything could happen. Hmm, that wasn't just at HQ. That was my life now. I was getting used to the unpredictability… although, in a way, the unpredictability was predictable, so one could argue that there really was no unpredictability. Well, it made total sense in my head.

Liv and I arrived at the same time as Beren. Oops. "Oh, Liv," I said. "I forgot to tell you that Beren will be at your office at five thirty, and he said to tell you hello."

Beren shook his head. "You're hopeless, Lily. I could tell her myself now."

"I know. But I would've remembered eventually. I just hadn't had time."

"Hadn't had time to remember?" Beren raised a brow.

"Well, we started eating pretty much straight away, and well, I forgot. Food makes me do that."

"Blaming food, Lily? That's a new low, even for you." His lips upturned on one side let me know he was joking.

Liv put her arm around me. "Lily would've told me, eventually. Probably when you were knocking on the door at five thirty… but still." She giggled, and I swatted her arm off my shoulder.

"And you call yourself a friend. Pfft." I took a seat at the conference table to the right of Will. Ma'am was at her usual spot at the head of the table, my brother on her left, Millicent next to him—she was working again while we cleaned this mess up, but since she hadn't been in her office, I had to assume Ma'am was keeping her busy elsewhere. Liv sat next to me and Beren next to her. At the foot of the table sat a very sexy Agent Viking, the one who'd driven us to the gallery. Ma'am cleared her throat. I blushed. *Oops.* I turned to her. *It's not a crime to look.*

She narrowed her eyes. I shrugged. I loved Will for who he was, and I thought he was hunky too. I could guarantee that he took notice when a gorgeous woman walked past. He was only human. There was no way I'd leave him for anyone or anything, and he knew it. I was betting Ma'am knew it too, but she just enjoyed giving me a hard time. She smirked. Argh!

"Where's Imani?" I asked. She was normally at these meetings because she was someone Ma'am trusted implicitly, and so she should—Imani had sworn to protect me to the death, and it was binding. She was definitely on our side.

"She's out in the field, dear. And before you ask, it's on a need-to-know basis. Now let's get started." She gave Agent Lyon a nod, and he made a bubble of silence. A weird yearning twisted my gut. I missed calling on my magic. As well as saving time and effort, it made me feel accomplished and powerful, like I could take on anyone, do anything, and now it was denied me. At the risk of stating the obvious, I hated having my favourite things taken away. For the first time in this whole curse thing, anger simmered in my belly.

"Thank you, Agent Lyon. Right, as you may have heard, Dr Finnegan and his nurse have gone home sick. We're not sure if it's related to the curse or not. We haven't had any other reports of healthy agents coming down with anything, but as we can't afford to lose anyone else, we're having our healthy agents use protection spells when they're with cursed agents. This uses a fair amount of power, and it's going to put a drain on our resources, yet again." At this rate, the PIB would be out of business in a month. How could agents do their jobs with only their talent distinguishing them from a non-witch? Hmm, I guess it was doable, but you'd have to send a group of agents to handle everything, rather than just one or two, and anyone working undercover by themselves would be at a distinct disadvantage.

"Agent DuPree, I want you to undertake a health check on all our uncursed agents. I know it's going to take time, but we need to know for sure if this thing is spreading."

"Yes, ma'am."

Ma'am's phone rang. She frowned and answered it. "What is it?" A flash of incredulity widened her eyes before she reined it in and resumed her poker face. "Secure the facility. I'll be right there. Is the landing spot still safe?" She listened and nodded a couple of times. "Mmhmm. Right. Bye." She looked at Millicent. "I need you to take me to Spellford Jail. There's been an explosion and fatalities, but we don't have an accurate number yet." She stood and addressed the rest of us. "I'm sorry, but this meeting is over. We'll reconvene at six tonight. Agent Lyon, please meet us at the facility." He nodded and stood.

Millicent also stood and moved away from the table. She made a doorway. Ma'am walked through, and after James shot Mill a goodbye-be-careful look, Millicent stepped through and disappeared. Then Agent Lyon made his doorway and was gone in an instant. The rest of us watching worriedly. Being unable to help really sucked. Were they walking into the aftermath of something or just the beginning? Goosebumps raced along my arms.

"Is there anything we can do?" Liv asked James.

"I'm afraid not. Just keep going with whatever you were working on before. Agent Blakesley, can you help me coordinate the disaster protocol from here? Ma'am's going to need support, information, and assistance."

"Of course. Just tell me what I need to do."

"And Agent DuPree, I'd say you'd best get started screening our healthy witches."

"Will do." Beren stood and turned to Liv. "I'll be by to pick you up later, but best make it six thirty."

Liv nodded. "Not a problem."

Liv and I waited until everyone had gone before we got to our feet. Even though paperwork and research were important, what we were working on wasn't going to solve anything quickly. I bit my fingernail. Surely there was something we could do to really help. Hmm, what if I managed to weed out who had cast that spell this morning when the second message came through? I could do it with my phone so I didn't look too suspect wandering around. The only problem would be if the security cameras were manned by someone who was involved.

I looked at Liv. "Can I borrow your notepad and pen?"

"Sure." She handed them to me, curiosity shining from her eyes.

"I need to go to the bathroom before we head back. Wanna come?" Yes, weird question, and I wasn't one of those people who needed company in the bathroom—in fact, I hated anyone listening to what went on in the bowl. But I had a good reason this time. Honestly.

Liv's forehead furrowed for a moment, but then she opened her mouth in an "ah." "Yeah, sure." I loved that I could always count on my best friend.

In the bathroom, I pointed to one cubicle, and then I went in the one next to it. I put the toilet seat down and sat to write in the notebook. The toilet was the only place in the PIB that was surveillance free—at least I assumed so. Hmm, maybe I should check. "Hang on a minute, Liv."

"Yeah, sure."

I put the notebook on my lap and pulled out my phone, then turned on the photo app. I spoke in my mind. *Show me any cameras.* I panned around where I could see—nothing. I picked up the notebook, opened the door, and with the camera in the other hand, panned around the bathroom. Nothing. Phew.

I hurried back into my stall and sat again. Placing my camera on my lap and notebook on top of it, I wrote a note to Liv.

I want to see if I can find out who cast the message spell to Ma'am this morning. It was someone inside the PIB. But I'll look weird running around taking photos. Can you come with me, and I can pretend I'm taking photos of you? I'm not sure what story we'll have for that though. What do you think? Oh, and I've checked for cameras in here, and there aren't any.

I slid the notebook and pen under the small gap under the divider into her cubicle.

After a couple of minutes, the notebook came back.

That's a great idea! Maybe we could pretend we're doing an audit of the premises for Ma'am—making sure fittings and furniture etcetera are all up to standard and checking what we need to budget for next year. You could just video as we're walking. We might need to clear it with Ma'am first, though, because we'll need access to everyone's offices.

Ooh, she was clever, and she made some good points. I wrote another message.

Maybe I could get clearance and a letter from James to take around since he normally speaks for her. And he's here. I think Ma'am has way too much on her plate for us to bother her. If I called her now, she'd likely say no because she'd be annoyed at the interruption.

I slid it under the partition. A minute later, it came back.

Sounds good. Let's go find James and ask. And while you're filming, I'll hold a notebook and pretend I'm taking notes.

I flushed the toilet, just in case anyone happened to be in the bathroom—not that I'd heard anyone coming or going, but you never knew, especially around witches. Liv and I washed our hands, then went to find my brother.

James was a reasonable guy, but what if he said no because he didn't want me to get in the middle of anything? Once that happened, I wouldn't be able to go over his head to Ma'am—kind of like when one parent said no and you went to the other parent. That just led to a whole lot of trouble. I guessed the worst that was going to happen if he said no was that we wouldn't be able to help, which would be frustrating, but it wasn't life-threatening.

We found him in the sickbay with Beren and one of the healthy witches, who was saying goodbye. After they left, James asked what we were doing.

"Here." I handed him the notebook. "Just read it." I shifted my weight from foot to foot as he read. *Please say yes.*

Please say yes. He handed me back the notebook. "Come with me. I think I have a job for you."

Liv and I looked at each other and shared a smile. Victory was ours. Now we just had to make it count.

James strode down the hallway, and we caught the lift to the floor below. We got out and turned right till we came to a branching and went left. And there was his office. He unlocked it, and we followed him through the reception area that all the offices here seemed to have, and he motioned for Liv and me to sit in the guest chairs in front of his table.

He sat and magicked paperwork into being on his desk. James was lucky he hadn't been inside the building when he came to help heal dizzy witches the other day. The curse seemed to have mainly affected any witches who'd been inside. A couple of the witches who'd only been outside were affected but not as badly as the rest of us.

James handed me two pieces of paper. "Here's the paperwork authorising the audit. Make sure you get pictures of everything: carpet, blinds, chairs, tables, etc." He winked at me. "I'll make sure we have a list of company laptops and desktops. If anyone needs an upgrade, I'll include that, so don't worry about those things."

I saluted. "Yes, boss."

"You'll need this." James held out his hand to me, and a key appeared in it. "It's the master key to every office. Just make sure you knock first—we don't want to upset anyone by barging in. Okay?"

"Yep." I took the key.

"And if anyone gives you a hard time, tell them to call me."

"Will do." I mouthed, "Thanks."

He smiled. "Now off you two go. I want a report on my desk by tomorrow afternoon. You have a lot of ground to cover, and stick to ground, first, and second floors." He gave us a stern look.

"Of course. We'll make sure we hand in a thorough report." I gave him a wave, and Liv and I left. She had her notepad and pen at the ready. "Do you want to start on the ground level and work our way up?"

"Sounds logical."

Out of all the offices on the ground floor, fifteen were empty, which was great, one had an agent in a dog suit— apparently he'd tried to magic his dog to headquarters, but it went wrong, surprise, surprise—and ten had normal agents doing normal things. Not one office showed me anything out of the ordinary. Maybe my plan wasn't going to work. Not that I was going to give up. But my magic use had drained me. Because I couldn't draw any river magic, I was depleting my natural stores. Talents were the only spells where you could use just your own internal store of energy, but in doing so, you paid a hefty price. But we needed to find out who was doing this as soon as possible. So I kept going.

We were halfway through the first floor when Liv's phone rang. Looking at the screen, she said, "It's Ma'am." She answered it. "Hello, Liv speaking." Phone calls rarely boded well. "Ah huh. Okay. Yes. Bye." Liv hung up and looked at me. "You have to return to James's office. You're required out in the field."

"Oh." I blew out a breath. "I suppose we can get back to this later." I shivered. In the meantime, there was another mole running around the PIB. Was it the person who had cursed us, or was it an accomplice? And how far were they willing to go? My shoulders slumped. We weren't safe anywhere anymore, except maybe at home, thanks to Millicent's dad.

Liv left me at her office, and I continued on to James's. I knocked, then entered. "Hey, brother of mine, what do you need?"

He looked up from his laptop. "Hi, Lily." He magicked a bubble of silence. "I'm going to take you to the prison. Ma'am wants some photographs. You've got your Nikon here? We need it to look official, so take some real photos too, and we'll put those on the system as part of the investigation. Our forensics team is there too. The scene is rather… messy."

I swallowed. *Messy* meant bodies mixed in with the debris. Yuck. But Ma'am had said there were casualties, so it was to be expected. "I'll have to go and grab my camera from Liv's office."

"You do that, and I'll finish off this email. When you get back, we'll leave."

And that's what we did.

James's doorway opened to a concreted area in front of the jail on a temporary spot someone must have recently set up. Smoke haze drifted around, and I sneezed. A four-metre-high brick wall with razor wire on the top surrounded the compound. About one hundred metres away stood a sprawling yellow-brick two-storey building replete with guard towers. About a quarter of the front of it was a charred, smoking pile of bricks. People in forest-green uniforms helped PIB agents comb over the disaster. A couple of people were on stretchers and being attended to by white-clothed witches. When I looked with my second sight, their auras were glowing blue. The hum of their magic was barely noticeable at this distance, as was the magic from the other witches helping recover survivors.

James looked at me. "Ready?" I steeled myself, nodded, and we headed over.

Ma'am stood near the edge of the collapsed walls and directed the activity. As we reached her, she turned to a scrawny fifty-something woman whose scraggly salt-and-pepper hair flowed freely to her shoulders. If she'd been wearing a flowing dress rather than her agent suit, she would have looked like the traditional version of a witch. "Are you ready?" Ma'am asked. The agent gave a nod. "Give me ten minutes, and you can start."

"Yes, Ma'am."

Ma'am turned to me. "Lily, I'd like you to document the scene before we remove the bodies. I've had one of our team take some photos, but I want a backup, just in case." The meaningful look in her eyes told me all I needed to know, and besides, if she hadn't called me here to use my talent, what had she called me here for? Anyone could take a normal photo, and they already had.

"Yes, Ma'am." Before I could step towards the crumbling structure, Ma'am spoke to James.

"I'd like you to accompany her, please, Agent Bianchi. Make sure nothing falls on her."

He gave a quick nod. Then we headed for the debris. I bit my lip, hoping I didn't accidentally see any dismembered body parts. I've said it before, and I'll say it again: we don't give our emergency service personnel enough credit for what they have to witness.

I warily skirted the perimeter of the disaster. With each normal shot I took, I also took a second magical shot. My quiet request each time was "Show me who caused the explosion." Nothing unusual turned up until I had rounded the far corner of the building and was facing back towards Ma'am. A man wearing a black coat and balaclava appeared, feet spread and arms reached out above his head. Was it the same man I'd captured all the other times? I took a couple of wide shots and then zoomed in to get more details. I also walked a bit closer, but I didn't want to get too close, or people would wonder what exactly I was photographing. The quality of the image would be high, so there would be no problem zooming in even further on the computer to get a look at his shoes, the only factor that could really tell us if it was the same guy.

I lowered my camera and said to James, "I'm done." We returned to Ma'am. She took a quick look at the photos, angling the screen so no one else could view them. When she finished, she handed my camera back and addressed the grey-haired agent next to her. "Agent Novak, please start."

Agent Novak took a deep breath and called upon her magic. The raw power of it surprised me, as did its dark undertones. But it wasn't evil… I didn't know what to think of it. It didn't creep me out, but it wasn't comfortable either. Her arms were stretched out in front of her, and she was making grabbing and pulling motions. The rubble shifted in one spot and collapsed in a puff of dust. A mangled body appeared on a white sheet of plastic laying on the ground to the right of Agent Novak. I gagged and turned the other way to avoid seeing more. A bit of warning would have been nice.

Each time the clink and scrape of bricks falling against each other came from behind me, I cringed. I'd counted four so far. How many people had died, and did I really have to stand here for the whole recovering-of-bodies thing? I shuffled backwards until I was facing my brother. His face tense, he gazed at the whole nightmare-inducing operation. I whispered, "Can we go now?"

He blinked and looked at me. "I'll check." He went to Ma'am and had a quiet conversation, then returned. "Yes. I'll take you back to headquarters." Just as he made a doorway, another man had appeared at our landing spot. Dressed in a dark suit but with a dark shirt rather than the white PIB shirt, he strode towards us, purpose and authority in every footstep, malevolence pulsing from him. Weirdly, he was wearing a black top hat.

James looked from the man to Ma'am and back again. "Come on, Lily. Let's go." Before I could object, he'd grabbed my hand and pulled me through his doorway and into the blessedly fresh air of the reception room, which was free of cloying smoke that leached the scent of burnt buildings and charred bodies. I took the first non-shallow breath I'd had since we left.

I fell into one of the chairs, put my elbows on my thighs and head in my hands.

"Are you okay, Lily?"

"I'm just tired. It's been a long day." I looked up and gave him a wan smile. "I'll be okay after a night's sleep. And what was with that guy? You got us out of there pretty quickly." James regarded me with a closed mouth. His lips twitched as if he were about to open his mouth and tell me, but he stopped when Gus opened the door and poked his head in.

"Hello, Agent Bianchi, Miss Lily. Do you want to come out, or would you like a moment?"

I knew the conversation was over. Whatever was going on was beyond my knowledge, at least until tomorrow—nagging required more energy than I had right now. I hoisted myself off the chair with a grunt. What an effort. Had my body doubled in weight since before we left? I knew it hadn't, but fatigue had its mean little claws in me, trying to drag me down. James cocked his head to the side, his eyes concerned. "Maybe I should take you home. You don't look the best."

"I'm fine, really. Just exhausted."

James turned to Gus. "I'll be back soon. I'm just going to take Lily home."

"Good idea." Gus winked, pulled his head back out, and shut the door.

"Come on. You're no use to anyone when you're like this."

Too tired to argue, when he made his doorway, I gladly shuffled through.

CHAPTER 10

After getting home late yesterday afternoon, I ate some cheese on toast—the easiest thing to make with my non-witch skills—I fell into bed and slept until the next morning when Will gently shook my shoulder. "Lily, wake up."

I reluctantly squinted my eyes open. "What time is it?"

He sat on the edge of the bed, already dressed in his uniform. "Eight."

Although he was ready for work, he looked like he should be going back to bed. The dark puffiness under his eyes was clear, even in the dim light. "What time did you get in last night?"

"Midnight. We've got too much on. That's why I'm getting you up now. Emergency meeting's been called at your brother's, seeing as how last night's was cancelled."

My eyes opened all the way, and I sat up so quickly, my

head spun. "What happened? Is everyone okay?" Gah, it was too early for a racing heart.

"I have no idea. Just hurry up and get ready. Wear your uniform, just in case, and bring your camera."

"Okay." He stood so I could get out of bed.

"I'll see you downstairs. I've made coffee." He smiled.

"You're the best." I quickly dressed, washed my face, brushed my teeth—the usual things—then hurried downstairs. At least I'd had enough sleep, the fatigue of yesterday gone, shame the same thing couldn't be said about the heavy sense of dread tightening my shoulders and jaw.

Ma'am was downstairs already, and had, in fact, finished her tea and breakfast. As I walked in, she was shutting the dishwasher. She turned around. "Good morning, dear." Dressed in her usual perfectly pressed uniform, her hair in its tidy bun, the only sign of the latest stress was… well, there wasn't any. How did she hold things together so well? I was betting she was like the duck who looked calm on top of the water, but her mind was as busy as those little webbed feet under the water. That made me think of Will's car. Despite the potentially dangerous or depressing day ahead, I couldn't stop the grin.

"Morning."

"What are you so happy about," she asked.

"I just remembered the quackmobile."

Angelica smiled. "At least we have something to smile about."

Will handed me a green to-go coffee cup. "You can

drink this on the way." Wow, so he still couldn't smile about his car.

"It's not like the Range Rover won't be changed back as soon as Angelica has her powers working properly. I'll be sorry to see the duck go. I feel like we've bonded." All I got for my efforts was a bland stare. I snorted.

"Okay, children. Time to go." Angelica led the way outside to her car. Oh, another gloriously freezing day of drizzle. At least winter couldn't last forever, and it was February. Spring would soon be here, and hopefully better times with it.

The drive to my brother's was a fairly quiet one, Angelica giving no hint as to what we were about to discuss. Several times I opened my mouth to ask but then remembered we didn't have a bubble of silence. Ultimate-patience mode activated.

As we drove, my stomach rumbled. I'd finished my coffee, but my lack of forethought about breakfast was a mistake I was paying for. The last thing I'd eaten had been at about six last night, and one sandwich wasn't really much of a dinner. Thankfully, as soon as we walked into James and Millicent's, the fragrance of bacon and eggs enveloped me along with my sister-in-law's hug.

After greetings and breakfast, Millicent magicked the plates away, and we got down to business. Apart from Will, Ma'am, and me sitting at the table, Beren, Liv, James, Millicent, and Imani were there. My heart vibrated with warmth at being surrounded by those I loved most. It was a miracle we were all safe and well, considering what we'd been through in the last ten months. I was taking that as a win.

I looked to the left at Ma'am, who spoke from her place at the head of the table. "I'm sure I don't need to say this, but what we speak about and do here today is to be kept under the utmost confidentiality. Am I understood?"

We all answered, "Yes, Ma'am." It normally went without saying. What had gotten her so spooked that she required an extra promise? I was betting that man from yesterday as James and I left had something to do with it.

Ma'am met my gaze, but I wasn't sure what she was thinking as she briefly stared into my eyes. She broke eye contact and looked towards the foot of the table at Millicent. "We've had an extremely generous offer from Millicent's father, Robert. Last night, he agreed to look into the curse for us. He and Beren have been working on a cure all night." We all looked at Beren. Dark circles dirtied the skin under his eyes. His tie was missing, and his shirt was open at the collar. He gave a wan smile. "Thanks for your commitment, Agent DuPree. They haven't cracked it yet, but by all accounts, they're close. Our plan is to cure those around this table first, but I don't want anyone else knowing." She turned to me. "And before you ask, Lily, I don't want anyone finding out. There's a mole at headquarters, and the criminals we're trying to catch will be at a disadvantage if they don't know we have our powers back. Let them stay cocky and make a mistake. Once we're at full power, it will be much easier to close in on them. They would never have gotten this far if they hadn't disabled us." That was definitely something I could agree with.

Ma'am smoothed her hair with her palm, then settled her hands in her lap. "Because we can't use our mind shields, we're also going to avoid being around other agents at all costs, except for Millicent and James, who, of course, aren't affected."

Damn. How was I supposed to unearth the culprit's mole at the PIB? I'd only gotten halfway through my search yesterday. I raised my hand.

"Yes, dear?"

"How are you going to stay away from the PIB? I mean, aren't you the boss?"

As calmly as you pleased, she replied, "Not anymore, Lily. I've been suspended, as of yesterday."

My mouth dropped open, and there were several loudly sucked in breaths. At least I hadn't been the last to know this time. Small consolation, really.

Anger simmered in Will's eyes. "That's ridiculous!"

James looked at Will. "One of the directors was there yesterday." He turned to Ma'am. "I'm right, aren't I? That man in the top hat. Which one is he?" Wow, seemed as if their identities were super top secret. But why had he then waltzed on in, in so public a fashion?

She lifted her chin and sniffed. "I only know him as Mr Brosnan. He came yesterday, took me to their secret offices. I was given my suspension by the big boss, Mr Moore, then taken to headquarters to empty my desk. Brosnan supervised my clean out, then escorted me to my car, and that was it."

I put up my hand. My question was stupid, but I couldn't help it; I had to know.

"Yes, dear?"

"Brosnan and Moore… are they fake names? They sound like actors who played James Bond." It was ridiculous. I mean, who would do that? It was so cheesy—working for a spy organisation and wishing you were 007.

Ma'am's smirk was particularly vicious. "Yes. Their egos are way bigger than their reputations. But make no mistake: as stupid as they seem, they are powerful witches who will stop at nothing to get what they want. Being in the powerful positions they are takes more than hard work and intelligence. Politics and power are just as tied up in their jobs as any huge organisation. They have connections we can't even imagine—criminals, royalty, heads of governments, and wealthy corporations. I've suspected a couple of them have wanted me out of the way for a while, but I made my predecessor look good, so they kept me. And when Agent Pembleton died, I was the first choice because of my experience. But James and I are too honest to be in charge for long. Whoever's making the PIB look bad has played into their hands and given them the perfect excuse to ditch me."

"So James won't be promoted in your stead?" asked Millicent.

"I doubt it. If he was, it would be better for all of us."

Mill and James shared a worried look. My brother drummed his fingers on the table. "Who do you think they'll get? Will it be someone I can work with? Maybe I should go undercover, pretend I'm happy you've been let go. When are they going to make the announcement?"

Ma'am shot her flinty gaze over each of us in turn. "The rumours have likely already started. Quite a few agents saw me marched through headquarters yesterday. I can see them parading someone in there today and announcing they're in charge. Prepare yourselves. James and Liv can go, but the rest of you are to call in sick. Not only are we fighting the PIB's enemies, we're fighting for the survival of the organisation. Something's going on, and we're going to discover what it is."

Crap. Now there was no way I could find out who was helping the curser. And as if we needed something else to figure out and fix. Why couldn't we just walk away from the whole thing? Oh, that's right—without the PIB's resources, we likely would never find out what happened to my parents or bring those responsible for their disappearances to justice. We could probably ask the PIB to investigate, but without Ma'am or James running things, they were likely to say it was such an old case and they didn't have the resources. RP was powerful too, and if we tried to take them down without agency backup, we'd lose. I was sure of it. Not to mention the moles in the PIB. It was essential that we had people on the inside.

Plus, my brother, his wife, and my friends needed jobs.

"Anyway, I'm not fired yet, and I won't make it easy for them. I have an idea who on the board of directors is pushing for my demise, and now I'm not required at work, I have time to untangle this mess, which is their first mistake. But having my magic—and all of you having yours—is essential to solving my problem, and to bring the perpetrator of our curse to justice. I'm sure I don't have to ask, but who's with me?"

I smiled and shot my hand in the air. "Me!" Liv did the same, and everyone else answered in the affirmative but without the vigorous arm actions.

Ma'am grinned. "Thank you. I knew I could count on all of you. Now, let's get on with this."

⊱✦⊰

AFTER THE MEETING, WE DROVE HOME AND SPENT THE REST of the day discussing, researching on the net, and planning for when we had our magic back. It was with great frustration that Will, Angelica, and I sat on the Chesterfields and listened when James visited that night with news.

James sat opposite Angelica. He rubbed a palm up and down his thigh. This wasn't going to be good. "They've replaced you with a guy from the US—Agent Chad Williamson the Third." His hand stilled on his leg, and he looked as if he was holding his breath.

Ma'am's jaw clenched, the muscles bunching. Her chest expanded with a large, slow breath. It went on for so long, I wondered whether she was going to explode. When she finally reached capacity, she opened her mouth and spoke… loudly. "That moron! What were they thinking? He botched that case last year in New York. Ten of our best agents died because of his incompetence. He wouldn't know how to run a cake stall let alone an agency headquarters. Are they trying to insult me?" Her nostrils flared. "And what's wrong with our own agents? Why did they have to import someone? It's not like I don't have a whole bureau full of agents who could do the job better than him." She waved a hand in my direction. "Lily would be better than him, for goodness' sake."

I opened my mouth to protest the unfairness of that statement—even though I hadn't the slightest idea of how to run the PIB—but Will shook his head. I narrowed my eyes. I understood she was upset, but why did she have to insult me every chance she got?

She looked at me. "Sorry, dear. I was just making a point. You're wonderful, and we couldn't do without you, but you running headquarters would be ridiculous."

I rolled my eyes. Whatever. Time to get the focus off my incompetence. "Why would they do that… replace you with someone so terrible?"

Angelica folded her arms. "Either they're even more moronic than I thought, or someone has an agenda."

"I'm voting option two. Notwithstanding his incompetence, if they'd chosen an agent from here, they'd risk having someone in charge who was faithful to you." Will rested an ankle on his knee as he relaxed back into the couch. "The better question is, what are we going to do about it?"

My brother stood. "I'll have to get going, but I'll check in with Rob tonight. B texted earlier, and he's having a sleep before getting back to finding a solution later tonight. He says they're close."

I wanted relief to sweep through me, but it wouldn't come. With everything going wrong, it was difficult to believe even this would go right. But sometimes you had to have faith because it was all that was left.

CHAPTER 11

The next morning, Angelica and Will had their heads together over the kitchen table, discussing things. I wasn't invited, so I took my breakfast into the TV room. When I switched on the TV, it happened to be news time. A blonde female reporter, red beanie and scarf bright in the morning grey, spoke into her microphone while standing on the footpath. Was that the main street of Westerham? I leaned forward—not that I needed to. The pet shop was clear in the background.

The bright lights of emergency services flashed in the background and reflected off shop windows. The reporter asked a tall, youngish man next to her a question. "There were reports of lightning strikes. Is that true?"

The man nodded quickly, his hazel eyes wide. His thick cockney accent made him difficult to understand. "It was unbelievable. Crash, boom, crash. I 'eard five of 'em. And the light! So bright. 'appened so quick, too, like. I shut me eyes, and when I opened 'em, there's five people dead on the footpath. Crazy stuff." He shook his head, bewildered.

"You're obviously lucky to be alive. Are you going to buy a lottery ticket?"

He chuckled. "Yeah, man. I should, eh. Me and the lads should go for a pint later too. It was freaky as." He put his hand on his black beanie and shook his head. A thick gold band on his ring finger with a large dark-green square stone in the middle gleamed starkly against the black of his head covering. His wife was going to be so relieved he was okay. It really was their lucky day, but what were the chances of five lightning strikes killing five people.

Weird.

That guy didn't know how lucky he really was. Had Angelica's antagonist struck again?

The reporter looked into the camera. "Unfortunately, the five victims didn't have such a lucky escape. Authorities are now working to identify them and notify family members. Back to you in the studio, Leigh."

I put my coffee on the small table next to the couch and hurried upstairs to grab my phone. I texted James.

Did you hear about the lightning strikes this morning? Five strikes, five dead. Could it be the same people as the curse?

His reply came five minutes later.

I don't know. I've just arrived at work. Will check it out and get back to you.

Okay, but be careful xx.

I worried my bottom lip with my teeth. Would James be a target at headquarters because he was clearly one of Ma'am's favourites? Would they find a way to fire him too? Now more than ever, he had to tread carefully. Anger burned in my chest. Why was it always the good people who were shafted? Why did horrible people usually win? Probably because they didn't care what they had to do to get ahead. Not having a conscience was like being a hot-air balloon without weights to hold it down. The heights one could reach when they didn't have that holding them back...

Well, maybe I could become that weight holding them to account. Once I got my magic back to normal, they'd better watch out. I stood and went to the window to spot some squirrels—if Angelica picked up on my thoughts, she'd likely put a kibosh on my efforts. The less she knew, the better, and what more wonderful way to distract myself than with the cute little critters.

As I stared out the window, an overwhelming urge to feel my magic cascaded over me. The river of power could be intoxicating—the tingly warmth that energised my whole body and mind. The anger I'd experience earlier intensified. How dare they do this to us! Rob us of who we were. I took a deep breath and opened myself to the golden river. Immediate calm embraced me from the inside out. Surely it couldn't hurt. It wasn't like I was casting a spell with it.

A squirrel dashed up the tree, and I grinned. So cute!

Imagine if they were bigger—like human-sized—how cuddly they'd be. It would also be cool if they could talk to us; ah, the conversations we'd have. Magic flowed through my veins. The squirrel turned towards me, and our gazes connected.

My eyes widened as the heat of power travelled from my core to my chest, down my arms and out of my hands. But I hadn't asked it to. I tried to close the portal, but it stayed open, magic pouring through.

Crap.

Racing footfalls echoed through the house. Will burst through the doorway, followed closely by Ma'am. "Lily, are you all right? What's going on?"

"I—I didn't mean to do anything. I just wanted to feel my magic, and now it won't stop." A flicker out the window caught my eye.

Oh. My. God.

My magic finally stopped flowing. I shut down the portal, but the rest of me stood frozen. What had I done? Was it entirely bad? I cocked my head to the side. Nah, it was okay. Surely, it wasn't the end of the world.

Angelica and Will joined me at the window. Ma'am was the first to find her voice. "What in heaven's name have you done?"

Will opened his mouth to speak, but only a squeak came out. His slack mouth stayed open.

Maybe if I acted calm, they'd see that it wasn't all that bad. I shrugged. "It could be worse." Before they could disagree, I ran to the front door and outside. Standing in front of the other magical mishap—the quackmobile—its eyeline level with mine, was the animal I'd accidentally made into the Godzilla of squirrels. Oops.

Huge, round, dark eyes stared at me. I suppressed a nervous giggle. It was soooooo cute! Except its claws were bigger, dangerously so. As much as this was my dream come true, I'd better be careful.

Making sure my voice was soft, I said, "Hello. I'm Lily. Um… sorry about this. It was an accident."

The squirrel made a *muk, muk* sound. It calmly moved its head from side to side, taking everything in. It was probably thinking how weird it was.

I tried again. "Can you talk?" Noise rustled behind me —Angelica and Will carefully approaching.

The squirrel didn't answer, but Will did. "Of course it can't talk. You've created a giant normal grey squirrel."

My shoulders sagged. How disappointing. "Oh. I wasn't sure because when I was thinking I'd love it to be cuddle-sized, I also wished it could talk."

Angelica folded her arms. "I wouldn't call that cuddle-sized, dear, unless you enjoy cuddling bears. Whatever you've done, dear, until you can undo it, we'd better get it inside. If someone sees this, how are we supposed to explain? And the last thing I need is for the PIB to come and arrest one or all of us for performing magic in public and drawing attention to ourselves."

"If it can't understand me, how are we supposed to get it inside?" Not to mention the damage a manic squirrel could do when it weighed 140 pounds. I stepped closer to it—I really, really wanted to give it a hug, or at least a pat. Surely that would be okay? It wouldn't suddenly be violent just because it was huge.

The squirrel's tail twitched and flicked from side to side before it turned and scampering back up the tree, although it lumbered more than scampered, if I was honest. Climbing trees was obviously easier when you weighed a few grams rather than tens of pounds.

Angelica put her hands on her hips. "*Now* look. Honestly, as if I don't have enough problems." She pulled out her phone and dialled. "Hello, James? Can you please come over—we have an emergency. Thank you." She gave me a narrowed-eye stare and shook her head. I gave her my best "what are ya gonna do?" look. She rolled her eyes.

Will moved to the bottom of the tree and stared up. The squirrel sat on a sturdy branch, thank goodness. I doubted it had realised what being bigger and heavier meant, and since it hadn't developed the excellent skill of conversing, I couldn't explain. "Maybe we should get Millicent here instead. She can talk to it." Millicent's talent was talking to animals, even ones that weren't special in any way… not that a giant fluffy squirrel wasn't special.

"Why don't you call her, dear? I'm going to answer the reception-room door. Both of you, watch that thing. If it comes down, get it in the house."

Will's forehead scrunched into lines. "How do you propose we do that? It's got huge claws and teeth."

"Ask your girlfriend. She's full of good ideas." With that, she turned and strode back inside.

Will raised a brow at me. I shrugged again. My shoulders were getting a real workout today.

Uh-oh, trouble at twelve o'clock. Old Mrs Soames from across the road was on our side of the street and closing fast, well, as fast as one can when they're ancient and short. A few months ago, we'd rid her home of witchy ghosts. Her gratefulness at our help had diminished over time, and she was back to her crabbiest self. She stopped in front of Will. "What's going on out here? There's no trouble, is there?" *Please don't look up. Please don't look up.*

Will put on his most nonchalant expression. "No, of course not. We're thinking of redoing the garden in spring. Just discussing the logistics of where we should put what."

She narrowed her eyes and gave him a slow nod that reeked of suspicion. Her gaze travelled to the quackmobile. "And what is that? Are you going into business selling bath toys? Because I don't think it's lucrative. That's a sure way to lose all your money, and I'm sure Lily doesn't want to marry a man with dismal prospects." Oh, God, had we fallen into a time-travel portal and gone back to the eighteen hundreds?

Will was a quick thinker—I'd give him that. "Ah, no, Mrs Soames. My friend is away. This is his car, but it doesn't fit in his garage, so I'm minding it till he gets back."

She sniffed. "What strange friends you have, William." She turned, surveying everything, eventually making it back around to stare at me. "And you're sure everything is fine?"

I gave her my best "everything is fine" smile. "Definitely. Couldn't be finer. How's Ethel?" Ethel was her loud, annoying cockatoo, which she loved very much. It was such an easy way to redirect the conversation, although I didn't want her standing there talking all day. What if the squirrel came back down?

Her face softened. "Ethel is very well, thank you for asking." Unfortunately, she was more switched on than the average elderly neighbour, and her expression sharpened as she peered past me before looking at me again. I did my best not to look up in the tree to ascertain the squirrel's position. "You're sure everything is okay?"

"Yes, Mrs Soames. If that changes, I'll be sure to let you know." My smile was increasingly hard to maintain. Could she just leave already? Hmm… "To be honest, I'm not feeling 100 percent. I've had diarrhea this morning. Nasty bout, actually. Not sure if it's a virus or food poisoning." I rubbed my stomach.

Her face blanched. "Don't come near me, then. I'd best be going. Good day."

"Bye, Mrs Soames," Will and I said. As soon as her back was turned, I risked a glance up at the squirrel. Oh, crap.

It was gone.

Will looked up too. After a minute of intense staring, he said, "Where the hell is it?"

"I don't know. You'd think it would be easier to spot them when they're that size." He glared at me. I bit my bottom lip and resisted another shrug.

James, Millicent, and Ma'am came outside. They joined us at the tree, and James asked, "Where is it?"

Will took an annoyed breath through his nose. "Ask your sister."

Everyone stared at me, expectation on their faces, with the exception of Will and Ma'am, who were just irritated. "It's gone. At least, we can't see it in the tree anymore. It couldn't have gone far, and it'll be easy to spot." Okay, so let's not say anything about the fact that if it's too big for us to miss, everyone else is going to see it too....

Millicent put her hand up. "If everyone could just be quiet for a moment, I'll see if I can hear its thoughts. It shouldn't be too hard to pick out, considering it will likely be confused about its size." She shut her eyes. At least no one could tell me off while Millicent was concentrating. Disappointingly, Millicent opened her eyes. "It's gone that way." She pointed towards the house on the boundary next to the tree.

We all hurried to the grass verge in front of next door. I slapped my hand over my mouth. I wanted to laugh because seeing a giant squirrel on a roof was hilarious, but if any non-witches saw, we'd be in huge trouble, plus if Ma'am knew I was laughing, I'd get a two-day lecture.

As we stood, pondering, a voice came from behind us. "I *knew* there was something going on!"

Crap. Mrs Soames.

Ma'am spun around. "Hello, Mrs Soames. I'm afraid my nephew was visiting, and he has a terrible sense of humour. He's dressed as a squirrel and gone climbing. He's not all there, if you know what I mean." I cocked my head to the side and observed the squirrel. Would she really buy that? It looked way too real. A tingle of James's magic touched my scalp.

Mrs Soames looked up at the squirrel, squinted, pursed her lips, then blinked. "Why didn't someone just say? Right. Well, I've wasted enough time on silliness today. I'm going home." Just like that, she turned and left.

I looked at James. "Did you just…?"

"Yes, but I had no choice. This could turn into a total disaster."

Millicent tucked blonde hair behind her ear. "If you can give me silence again, I'd appreciate it. I'm going to try and get the squirrel to come down and go inside. Does anyone have any nuts?" I looked at Will and snorted. He waggled his brows and grinned.

"Oh, for goodness' sake. Can't you take anything seriously, Lily?" Ma'am wasn't impressed, but what else was new?

"Sorry, couldn't help it. We do have some nuts, though. In the cupboard. Do squirrels like salted macadamias?"

"Yep," said Will, the resident squirrel expert. "Do you want me to go get them as a show of good faith to Squirrelzilla up there?" I snorted again. Why hadn't I thought of that name? Oh well, at least I could lay claim to naming the quackmobile.

Millicent nodded. "Get them but wait just inside the front door. I'm pretty sure I can get it to come at least that far. Its thoughts are a little scattered—as you'd expect—but it does understand me." Will left, and Millicent looked up at Squirrelzilla. The concentration on her face indicated she was talking to it. James, Angelica, and I watched in silence.

After some tail twitching, the squirrel scampered across the roof and leapt from the edge of it to the tree, which bent momentarily under its weight. No one must've been home because anything of that size traversing a roof would be noisy. Another small mercy.

As the squirrel descended, Millicent moved back to Angelica's driveway. We quietly followed. The last thing we wanted to do was scare it so that it ran down the street. Would it be possible to put a saddle on it? Wouldn't that be cool, riding a squirrel down the road! I didn't expect it would be able to carry someone up a tree though—the extra weight would be too much.

We all stayed at the end of the driveway waiting as Millicent and the squirrel approached the front door. The squirrel stopped and sniffed, its tail flicking. It jerked its head one way, then the other, and said, "Muk, muk, muk."

Millicent smiled and waited while the squirrel tentatively entered the house. Mill turned to us and gave a thumbs up. I smiled, sweet relief washing over me. Now I just had to hope it didn't scratch the furniture and make a huge mess. We didn't have magic to tidy it up with, and since all this was my fault, I'd be the one doing the cleaning. Maybe this wasn't so funny after all.

Once we were all inside, Will shut and locked the door. In the kitchen, Millicent fed the squirrel macadamias. I stood at the door, not wanting to spook it. I spoke quietly. "Can you tell it I'm a friend?"

Millicent chuckled. "I can tell it you pose no danger and that you're nice. They don't really have a concept of friends. This is just your garden-variety squirrel, not one suitable for being a familiar. Some animals have the capacity to understand us fully and converse properly, but not all." She handed it another nut and must have been telling it what I'd asked her to. It cocked its head to the side, looked at me, and sniffed. Adorable long whiskers twitched. "It says okay."

"I thought you said it wouldn't really understand much."

"It's talking to me in pictures and feelings. It gets that you're not a threat, and it's okay with you being near it."

"Can I pat it?"

Angelica stood behind me. "I can't believe we're having a crisis and this is what you're thinking about."

I turned around. "But squirrels. I love them. This is like a dream come true. I know we have a lot to deal with, but we always have some disaster or other to fix. If I don't get these moments, what's the point? And nothing's going to get worse if I have a minute or two patting a giant squirrel."

She sighed. "As much as this irritates me, you're right." She made a shooing motion with her hand. "Go and have your moment with the animal, then you're coming with James, Will, and me to his place." She was unusually calm all of a sudden.

Then realisation hit. My mouth opened in a wide O. We were going to get our magic back. Yippee! I calmed myself and turned back around. "So, is the squirrel okay with me patting it?"

Millicent smiled. "Yes, but no fast movements." She handed it a couple more nuts.

I quietly and unhurriedly—despite the acrobats of excitement flipping and somersaulting in my body—approached. When I was a foot away, the squirrel stared at me and stopped chewing. I whispered in one of those cute voices reserved for animal conversations, "Hey, little guy. It's okay. I won't hurt you." Okay, so it wasn't little anymore, but whatever. I ever so slowly raised my arm and let it sniff my hand.

Millicent handed me a few nuts. "Here. Offer him this."

Oh, it was a him. "Here you go." The squirrel took them from my palm with his clawed hands. I was practically vibrating with contained joy—refraining from squeeing and jumping up and down was super difficult. I took a deep breath. "I'm going to pat your back now." It looked at me, fluffy ears pointed towards me. Goodness knew what it was thinking, but I gently reached out, alert for any signs it was going to run. So far, so good. Then my palm was on its fur, stroking down. Soft, but not ridiculously so. It trembled. "It's okay, buddy." Not wanting to upset it, I gave it one last pat and backed away. "Thank you."

It went back to chewing macadamias. Angelica had a resigned expression on her face. "Come on. Let's go."

At the door, I waved. "Bye, squirrel. The next time I see you, I'll have to change you back. All good things must come to an end."

Millicent shook her head and smiled. "Get out of here, you goose. I'll see you later."

I gave her a cheesy grin and joined James and Angelica in the hallway. "I've already taken Will," said James. "Both B and Robert are unravelling this. They've pretty much been up all night. Robert will deal with Lily, and B, being younger and hopefully having more energy, will cure both Angelica and Will. But after that, they'll need a rest. We'll cure Imani tonight if Beren's up to it."

"Sounds good to me." I was keen to get my magic working properly. Being without it had caused way more trouble than I could have anticipated. And putting every-thing on hold in regards to RP was beyond frustrating.

James made his doorway, and I followed Angelica through.

THAT NIGHT, WILL, ANGELICA, JAMES, AND I SAT AROUND the kitchen table munching homemade pizza and garlic bread. The comforting aromas of our meal capped off what had actually been a successful day. Despite Squirrelzilla, everything had turned out well. Will, Angelica, and I had our magic back in full force, and the squirrel had been downsized to normal and was happily back with his buddies, darting about their business in anonymity.

James swallowed a mouthful of food. "Bloody Agent Williamson the Third told everyone you'd been fired over your continued poor handling of cases. He put Millicent and me on notice—said if we stepped out of line or conveyed any sensitive information to you, we'd be fired. He said, and I quote, 'I'll be watching you.'" He rolled his eyes. "The guy's an idiot. We had a call out today, and he didn't follow procedure properly. He pulled an agent off a case when she was close to finding out what we needed and stuck her somewhere else, for no good reason I could see. It's like he's trying to cause more trouble. I'd say I just don't get it, but I'm afraid I do."

Angelica, who'd hardly eaten anything, dabbed her mouth with her napkin. "Yes, the timing couldn't be better, could it? At this rate, we'll be shut down by Easter. I bet New York was happy to be rid of the incompetent moron. I wager he has no idea he's been moved here to ruin things rather than 'fix' them." She placed her napkin carefully on the table and shook her head. "I just can't understand it. We have supporters on the board of directors, enough that it shouldn't have gotten this far. What's changed?"

"You don't think RP managed to get to them somehow?" Will asked.

Angelica drummed her fingers on the table. "I wouldn't put anything past Dana, but they'd need tens of millions of pounds or some juicy blackmail material to take it this far. We've got support in the government, enough that they wouldn't look too kindly on us being disbanded. Without the PIB, there would be so much unsolvable witch crime, everyone would suffer."

I shuddered. Normal crime was bad enough. Left unchecked, witch crime would be catastrophic. Maybe that's how superheroes were created—when the authorities didn't do enough, you had to take matters into your own hands.

Not that any of us were remotely superheroish, although Angelica could be scary—I'd give her that. I smirked because she couldn't read my mind since I'd gotten my power back and put up my mind shield.

Angelica squinted at me. "What's so funny?"

My smirk grew to a grin. "Just enjoying the privacy of my own thoughts."

"Trust me, Lily, I'm extremely happy not to have to go there." She gave me a smirk of her own.

"Great! Now we're both happy." I picked up another piece of pizza and brought it to my mouth. As I took a bite, a piece of mushroom fell off onto my white T-shirt. I picked it off and put it in my mouth. It left behind a grubby mark —typical of me. Ooh, but now I could magic it off. Yay! I drew on my power and willed the stain away. It disappeared. Woohoo!

Ma'am smiled. "It's a relief, isn't it."

"You can say that again. In the early days, I didn't think I'd ever care whether I could use magic or not. It actually felt more like a burden than a gift, but now… I never want to be without it."

Warmth shone from Angelica's gaze. "I'm happy to hear that. Your mother would have been too. She was never quite sure how you'd go, being a witch. I know she sometimes felt guilty that she'd passed it onto you."

"Really? If I could see her now, I'd tell her I'm just proud to have something of hers. Wouldn't matter what it was. I'm glad I'm a witch."

James's smile held a tinge of sadness. "Me too, Lily. It

makes me feel closer to her in a way, you know? Closer to our heritage. I just want to make her proud, and Dad."

He was sitting next to me, and I grabbed his hand. "Me too." The thought that maybe they were still alive flitted through my head, but I batted it away—getting my hopes up was a sure way to have my heart broken all over again. They'd been gone so long that there was no way they were alive. If my mum was as powerful as Angelica said, she would have found a way out, and surely I would have felt her out there the same way I'd felt Will that time.

Angelica magicked her plate away, and a cup of tea appeared in front of her. Things really were back to normal. "As I see it, we have two problems, but with our small group, we may only be able to solve one at a time. The question is, which do we solve first? As much as I want my job reinstated ASAP, more damage is being done by whoever cursed us. I suggest we deal with that first."

James nodded. "I checked out those lightning-strike deaths from this morning, and there was definitely magic involved. I've kept it to myself, though. I'm sure Chad would find a way to turn it against us." He turned to me. "Now that you have your magic back, I think you should take photos of that scene. He had to be standing nearby when it happened. All we need is to see the guy in the dark coat, and we'll know."

"I can do that. Also, I haven't finished my audit of head-quarters. I'm sure I'd find who the mole is if I could just finish."

He shook his head. "It's too risky. There's no way to

sneak you in, and the new guy would shut anything down quickly if he thought Angelica had ordered it. You're not supposed to have a mind shield, remember? If anyone had their feelers out for thoughts, they'd know you blocked yours."

"Couldn't you just tell them that you blocked them for me?"

"I could, but…" James shared a meaningful look with Angelica.

She shook her head. "It's too dangerous. I don't want you exposed. If they catch you, they might confiscate your camera. We can't risk it. I think it's best if you photograph the lightning scene. Will can go with you. I have other things to organise, and they'll be on the lookout for me. I don't want to draw any attention to what we're doing, so I'm going to lay low. If we can solve this other crime, we'll find a way to work it in our favour with the board."

James's phone rang. He answered it. Yelling, in the form of a New York accent, came down the line. My brother held the phone away from his ear. "… blue light! What's the meaning of this message? Are they going to attack me personally? Why didn't you warn me? Get down here, now!" Yikes.

James rolled his eyes and put the phone back to his ear. "Ma'am had those messages before too. I'll be there shortly."

"You'd better be!" The line died.

James pocketed his phone. "I don't need to explain, obviously." He chuckled. "Not that it's funny, but it kind of is. I'll message you when I get home, let you know the result. I know it's cold, Lily, but there won't be many people around now. Can you and Will go take those photos?"

I shivered involuntarily. "Yeah, sure. It's not like we'll be out there long. Maybe we can pick up dessert from Costa while we're out." I turned to Angelica. "Would you like anything?"

"Not in the way of food, thank you, dear. Some enlightening photographs would be nice though." She smiled.

"I'm on it." I magicked my plate clean and away and stood. Will did the same. I clicked my fingers for fun. My coat appeared on my body and my camera in my hand. I grinned. I loved being a witch. Magic was where it was at, baby. The way our day was going, maybe, just maybe we'd get a case-busting clue tonight.

"Lily…" A warning tone from Will. "We may end up with nothing. Don't get ahead of yourself."

"How did you know what I was thinking? You can't read my mind, can you?" I checked my mind shield. It was up.

"I know you, gorgeous. You've got that look in your eye, and that cute little smile you don't even realise you're doing. As wonderful as your positivity is, it sometimes leads to crushing disappointment, so maybe let's go into this with no expectations. Okay?"

I unsmiled. "Fine." Getting my enthusiasm under control was one of my least favourite things to do.

Will led the way out the door, and the blinkers flashed on his car, indicating it was unlocked. Satisfaction played on his face as he looked at his car; then he glanced my way and raised a brow, daring me to say anything.

I wouldn't say I lived to disappoint anyone, but…

"I miss the quackmobile already." I opened the door, hopped in, and shot a pout his way.

He shut his door and did up his belt. Amusement twitched the corners of his lips. "I may have a surprise for you."

I sat up straight, like a dog who's just been told there's a walk on offer. "Ooh, did you make me one?"

He laughed. "No. Of course not. But I did get Angelica to save this." He pressed the horn. *Quack, quack, quack.* He waggled his brows. "You like?"

I giggled. "I love! Thank you!" We leaned towards each other and kissed. Will was totally a keeper. When we were done, I sat back and sighed. Today was definitely a good day.

It took hardly any time to drive into Westerham and the site of the lightning strikes. It had happened in front of two-storey terraced shops—one a pet shop, the other a vacant store. Will managed to find parking just around the corner, about seventy feet away.

I took the lens cap off the Nikon and turned it on. "I might just step back over here to see if he was standing nearby. Then I'll walk closer. Just make sure I don't walk in front of any cars." I was prone to distraction when using my talent, and the last thing I wanted was to step onto the road at the wrong time.

"Can do. I'll be watching out for anything and everything." He was probably talking about RP as well. We were never safe. It was a reminder to cast my return to sender, which I did. At least it had stopped raining, and a few stars peeked through between clouds. A couple of people walked along the footpath on the other side of the street, but it was fairly quiet—being eight thirty on a cold night, that was no surprise.

I lifted my camera to my face. "Show me who cast the lightning spells that killed five people."

Subdued sunlight illuminated the drizzly day, and I had to remind myself this was magic, not reality. Being effectively transported back in time was disconcerting when what revealed itself through the lens was far different from what I'd started with.

Standing, leaning with one shoulder against the wall, was the guy with the black beanie from the television interview this morning. The people who had been struck down were in the process of walking past him—two one way, three the other. Even though there were five people in my photo, I knew instinctively who'd done this—well, it wouldn't take Einstein since the guy with the black beanie had been the only one to survive, but my magical sense was insisting I focus on him.

And I could not believe our luck. I smiled, bubbles of excitement disturbing the calm within.

I walked towards where he'd been standing and took some close-ups. His expression was serious, almost angry. He'd definitely been on a mission. But why? And who was he? Did he know those people, or were they random? So many questions.

I lowered the camera and turned to Will. "Here."

He took the camera and looked at the screen. "I'm assuming it's the guy against the wall?"

"Bingo." He had some nerve too. "You know he was interviewed by the news this morning. He hung around and admitted he'd been at the scene. I can't remember whether he gave a name though. So damn brazen."

Will's eyebrows rose. "You're kidding?"

"Nope. He's been so clever, covering his tracks, but, of course, he had no idea about what we were capable of. Looks like he just made his first and, likely, last mistake." Sucked in, whoever you are. You're gonna go down. "He really fancies himself as some kind of criminal mastermind."

"Sure looks that way. Angelica's going to be ecstatic. Let's get going. The sooner we get this to her, the sooner we can try and find out who he is."

After a quick side trip to Costa, it took us next to no time to get home. We found Angelica reading by the fire in the living room. She waited until we were standing in front of her before she put the papers down and looked up. Her poker face relaxed slightly. "By the looks of you two, you have something good to show me?"

I grinned and handed her the camera. "You betcha. Check it out."

She scrolled through the photos. Her eyes widened. "Are you sure this is him?"

"My magic has never led me wrong. I was telling Will, that's the guy from the news this morning who was interviewed by the reporter. He had the audacity to thank his lucky stars that he was okay. He's just so smug, flaunting himself on TV, knowing the PIB might see it and not even realise. But he has no idea who he's dealing with." Two could play at the smug game, and I was feeling the smugness ooze from every pore. "Now all we have to do is find out who he is."

Angelica pursed her lips. "I doubt he gave his real name to the reporter, but we'll have to ask them anyway. You never know…. Can I get you onto that, Will?"

"Of course. I also think we should run his image through the system. Maybe get James to do it tomorrow. He kind of looks familiar, but maybe he has a common look. I've certainly never arrested him before."

"Neither have I, but you're right. There's something about him…."

I didn't believe it could be so easy, but it looked like we were close to solving this crime. "So once we find him, we just match his magic signature to the one at the crime scenes, and that's it?"

Will answered, "Yes and no. We'll need to tread carefully until we find out who his accomplices are. We want to catch everyone involved in this as soon as we can. If we miss anyone, they'll get off, and we'll never find them. We have to find out who he is and tail him for a while, bug his phone, house, etcetera. This could take a long time."

I folded my arms. "And in the meantime, Angelica's out

of a job, and you guys are risking everything. What are they going to do when you don't go back to work? They don't know you're cured, and because you don't know who the mole inside is, you can't risk going back. Same for Imani, assuming she's already cured, and Beren." I resisted the urge to scream. "There has to be some way I can figure out who the mole is."

Will wrinkled his forehead. "We can't risk any of us going back."

I sat in the other armchair near the fire. "I refuse to believe we can't do more. There has to be a way I can get in there and do what I need without getting caught."

Ma'am shook her head. "I'm afraid not, dear. We can't disguise you with magic because witches will see through that. I can't set anything up as an excuse or protect you now I'm not there. And I can assure you that whoever wants me gone will use any reason to get rid of your brother and Millicent. Too much is at stake, I'm afraid."

"Hmm, could we get James to say that in light of what happened, we're carrying out a security review? I could use a proper disguise, and maybe Gus could accompany me to photograph each room. James could say it's because of what happened, and we're ensuring everyone's safety—considering that guy was freaking out over more blue lettering. From what James said, he's stupid enough to fall for it. Taking it one step further, rather than say it came from you, we could possibly get James to convince the guy it's a great idea and to order it himself. He sounded spooked on the phone. It wouldn't take much for him to agree."

Angelica's smile was rather sharkish. "I like it, Lily. I think it could work. I'll contact James later, but be ready to report for duty tomorrow."

I grinned, and Will gave me a proud smile. "That's my Aussie witch, coming up with what we need at the right time. What would we do without you?"

A warning shiver skimmed down my spine. I hoped they never had to find out.

CHAPTER 12

The next morning at ten, I was ready. Imani—her power back in full force—had commandeered a make-up artist friend of hers to come and de-Lilyfy me.

Sam was about thirty. His shoulder-length dark dreadlocks framed a handsome face, his skin smooth and blemish-free. He had peachy cheeks that invited a squeeze... the ones on his face, obviously. I kept my fingers to myself though, as touching people without their permission was frowned upon. Those rounded cheeks rose to squint his brown eyes when he smiled, which he did often. He seemed to be a happy guy.

He'd fitted me with a red wig then formed the long locks into a bun, given me a slightly larger nose, brown contact lenses, and academic-looking black glasses. He'd even thickened my brows and extended them so they almost touched atop the bridge of my nose. It wasn't a look I'd repeat after this. Bushy brows and red hair didn't do me any favours. "This is practically a monobrow, Sam."

He laughed. "What better way to fly under the radar than have people look at you and comment on that? Your brows will steal the show. No one will think twice about whether you look familiar or not, and trust me—you don't look anything like you did before."

"Thank God I don't normally look like this." I laughed. At least it would be easier to get into character.

Imani handed me a small digital camera. "Use this. Half the agents have seen you running around with your Nikon. We don't want anyone to suspect anything."

I took it and placed it in a small, black handbag. "Thanks." I'd dressed in a white shirt and black, knee-length pencil skirt with sensible black court shoes and no tie—I didn't want to look exactly like an agent, but it had to scream boring and businesslike. We figured a no-nonsense look would best serve us.

Angelica stood and observed. She gave a nod. "Well done, Sam. Thank you for helping on such short notice."

"My pleasure. If there's anything else you need, let me know." He finished packing up his things, then turned to me. "Good luck, Lily."

I smiled and ignored the nerves bouncing around in my stomach. "Thanks."

A knock sounded on the reception-room door. "I'll answer it." It must be James. I couldn't wait to see his first reaction to my get-up. I unlocked the door and opened it.

His brow furrowed, confusion in his eyes; then he smiled. "Nice job! I didn't recognise you, but since there wasn't supposed to be any strangers here, I deduced it must be you." He shook his head. "Unbelievable." I grinned. "Now, that looks a bit like you. Maybe don't smile."

"Okay. Just let me get it out of my system now." The surest way to get someone to smile uncontrollably is to tell them not to. Or maybe I was just a rebel at heart.

"I'm just going to say hi to everyone." He strode into the living room. After some pleasantries, he said, "I can't tell you what I've agreed or said because I want Lily's reaction to be a surprise—it will be more believable." He turned to me. "You're a security consultant working freelance. You can't tell him who else you've worked with because it's classified. Oh, and can you sign this with your new name, Emily Black." A bound A4 document in a black folder appeared in his hand. I took it to the table, magicked a pen to myself, and signed my new name.

"Do I need ID?"

"Here." A small, black card with gold writing proclaimed my new name, occupation, mobile number, and PO-box address. "The only other people who know about this are Gus and his boss. I did a quick mind read to make sure they weren't in on anything." Angelica frowned. "I'm sorry, but I feel we have no choice at this point."

She sighed. "I suppose you're right, but we don't want to stop being professional."

"I'm doing my best." James's tone was firm but not disrespectful.

A tingle of James's magic feathered my scalp, then came a sensation as if someone was tapping a gentle finger against my forehead. I rolled my eyes. "Of course I have my mind shield up. I'm not about to make a stupid mistake like that. Trust me."

His expression remained serious, unapologetic. "I'm never going to leave anything to chance, Lily. We can't afford any mistakes."

Rather than roll my eyes—he was just trying to be safe—I shut my eyes and counted to three. Where did this mature Lily come from, and did I need to be worried the old me had disappeared? No. This was Emily Black, my staid, security-conscious alter ego. I smiled. "I'm ready. Let's get this over with."

Will gave me a quick kiss on the lips. "Be careful, Emily. If anything happened to you…" One corner of his mouth quirked up, creating a delicious dimple.

My stomach did a little flip. Even after a few months, he still had that effect on me. I hoped it would always be this way. "I will. You'd better be careful too." He gave me a quizzical look. "If Lily finds out about us, you're dead." I couldn't keep a straight face and laughed.

He laughed and shook his head. "I wouldn't doubt it. But she has nothing to worry about." He winked.

James grabbed my hand. "Come on. If I have to watch you two moon over each other anymore, I might just gag."

"You're such a baby. It's not like I haven't had to watch you be all smoochy with Mill."

He ignored my comment and made a doorway.

"Ready?" I nodded and stepped through into the PIB reception room. I pretended as if I'd never been there before, looking around and nodding—I was supposed to be taking note of security things after all.

James buzzed, and Gus opened the door. I caught myself just before I greeted him with a "Hello, Gus!" I kept a straight face until James introduced us.

"Gus, this is Emily Black, a security consultant. I'll be getting you to show her around, if that's okay."

"Of course, Agent Bianchi. It would be my pleasure." Gus held his hand out to me. "Lovely to meet you, Ms Black."

I gave him a close-mouthed smile. "Lovely to meet you too. Thank you. I appreciate it."

James ushered me into the hall while I gazed around like a newbie. I took my small camera out. I might as well start now. I thought, *Show me who put the messages in blue writing in Ma'am's office.*

Walking along the hallway, his back to us, was someone in a white coat. So, our culprit was a lab technician. It also appeared that my magic could show me who it was without showing me the exact moment they were doing it, although that would be more useful since I had to show it to Angelica later. I made my voice a bit lower—if I changed it too much, I would sound like someone being stupid. "Agent Bianchi, I've just spotted something down there. Mind if I check it out?"

"Of course. Please go ahead." Gus followed me. He didn't know about my talent, so he was probably wondering what I was up to. When I'd walked past the point of the person, I turned and pointed my camera back the way I'd come. Gus's face registered surprise, and he jumped out of the way. I stifled a chuckle. I repeated my request in my mind and looked through the camera.

Oh, crap.

My heart kicked into a gallop. This couldn't be right. Before I said anything to anyone, I wanted to confirm it. I took a couple of shots and composed my expression, so by the time I'd lowered the camera, nothing would seem amiss. To ensure I could confirm things, I needed to think about the most likely place he would have been when he cast the spell. Hmm… He would've had to know when Angelica would be in her office. Maybe he'd hung around and waited for her to go in, or maybe he had access to security cameras. Whatever it was, I'd just have to start in the most likely place. Once I asked, James would know who I was after. But what if the culprit was in his domain when we visited? I'd just have to deal with that when it happened.

"Ms Black, is something wrong?" James tilted his head to the side.

"Ah, no. Sorry. I'd like to start at the infirmary, if that's okay. I take it you have prisoners there sometimes?"

"Yes."

"Well, other than the reception room and the actual cells, that would be a room that requires extra security. Which way is it?"

"I think I'll come. Stay with us, Gus." My brother turned and headed for the lift. "Please come with me, Ms

Black." With James in front and Gus behind, I felt safe, but it could all be over if we ran into New York guy.

In the lift, I had to stop my foot from tapping. On the next floor, we got out and headed for the infirmary. Another two agents were walking towards us… I only recognised one of them, and by the tension that appeared in my brother's shoulders, the other one could be our worst nightmare. James managed to appear relaxed by the time our paths crossed. The person I didn't recognise lifted his hand in a stop gesture.

We halted. Damn.

His New York accent filled the corridor. "Agent Bianchi, what's going on here? Care to introduce me to your guest?" His bright-blue eyes regarded me. There was no poker face or malice going on. He looked genuinely curious. Kind of like when a child sees something interesting like a feather or shell. They just want to know what and why.

"Of course, Sir. This is Emily Black. Security consultant. Ms Black, this is our head of operations, Agent Williamson the Third."

I held out my hand and pushed my nerves away before they made my palm sweaty. "It's an honour to meet you. The head of the PIB, no less." I gave him the best "I'm so impressed I just might faint" smile with wide eyes. James's brows drew down. Maybe I'd overdone it and looked crazy rather than adoring.

Chad hesitated, then a satisfied smile graced his face, and he shook my hand. "Pleased to meet you, Ms Black." He turned to James. "Why are you showing a security consultant around? Headquarters is safe under my watch, you know." His relaxed demeanour changed as a frown made its way to his face.

James nodded. "Of course, Sir, but something you said made me think this would be a good idea. So, really, we have your brilliant foresight to thank. In fact, it's one of the better ideas that an HEO has come up with in years. I'm so glad you've been transferred here."

"Oh, thank you. I do try and be innovative. It's all part of the job." He smiled and nodded. "Carry on, then. Let me know how you go."

"Will do." James gave him a respectful nod, and I smiled. Gus stood silently next to the wall, looking like he wanted to blend in. I made sure to keep a relaxed expression until Chad and the other agent had disappeared around a corner. Knowing cameras were always watching, we maintained the façade.

"Can I see the infirmary now?" I asked.

"Of course, Ms Black. This way."

Not far down the hallway was the door we sought. It had its own intercom, which I'd not had to use before. There were a couple of large rooms behind the door, and if the doctor was treating someone in the far room, they might not hear feeble tapping. James pressed the buzzer. Dr Finnegan's voice answered as the lock buzzed. "Come in."

I followed James in, and Gus followed me. My mouth dried. Dr Finnegan would be the first person to see me who knew me fairly well. The agent with Chad was someone I'd only seen in passing. Because the doctor knew my voice, I'd also have to say as little as possible. Maybe I could pretend to be shy?

Dr Finnegan met us in the first room, which had white vinyl covered floors, a reception desk, and several chairs, just like a hospital waiting room. "Ah, Agent Bianchi." He shook James's hand. "What brings you here today? I hope no one's sick." He ran his gaze over me, then Gus. Thankfully, he didn't seem to recognise me.

"Nothing like that." James smiled, then nodded towards me. "This is Ms Black, a security consultant. Agent Williamson the Third has approved a security review in light of recent events. Ms Black is familiarising herself with headquarters. We're just going to have a quick look around. I hope we're not interrupting anything."

"Not at all. After all the drama we've had, there are no patients today. Things have settled down somewhat. Please, look around." He stepped to the side—not that his thin frame took up much room.

I took out my small camera and gave him a shy smile before quietly engaging my talent and pointing the camera around the room. When I was done, we went to the triage and treatment rooms. The first large room was where I'd been treated last time. The memories that returned were far from pleasant. But Dr Finnegan had done his best to heal me, and for that, I was grateful. It made what I was doing now that much harder. I pointed my camera and asked the question in my head, *Show me who sent Ma'am the messages in blue light.*

That was three times now. There was no way I could deny who it was.

Sitting on the side of one of the beds in my photo was Dr Finnegan, coat off. He had his eyes closed and may have been performing a spell. Unless I had video, it was impossible to tell. But it was definitely him. He'd been so loyal and had served the PIB well. What had made him help the enemy? Was it by choice or had he been threatened? Whatever it was, I wasn't about to ask him. I was keeping my information to myself until later.

After taking a few more non-important photos of the room, I turned the camera off, made my way to James, and said quietly, "I'm done."

We returned to the entry room. James gave Dr Finnegan a chin tip. "Thanks. We're done."

Rather than say goodbye, I waved as I slipped out the door in front of James and Gus. The sooner I got out of there, the better. While James showed me through the rest of the floor, I crossed my fingers that no one would ask to see my photos. Once we figured we'd covered enough of an area that it looked like we'd done a good job, I turned to James. "I have enough information now. I'll get started on devising an updated security plan tomorrow. I should have a comprehensive report to you within three to four weeks."

"That's excellent. Thank you, Ms Black." He shook my hand. Gus gave a smile.

"Lovely to meet you both. I'll be in touch." I made my doorway and returned to Angelica's reception room. Once I was safely at home, I sighed out a relieved breath. Guilt slowed my steps to the hallway. I was about to dob in a valued member of their team, someone who had likely helped all of us at one time or another. But it was for the best.

I wouldn't want to be Dr Finnegan when Angelica found out. I whispered my apologies into the empty air, not that this was my fault, but being the bearer of bad news was burdensome. How was that for a tongue twister? Leaving my regret in the reception room, I unlocked the door and stepped into the hall. "Hello! Anybody home?"

"In here," Will called from the living room.

I made my way through. Will was already standing, and he hurried over to give me a hug. "Are you okay? How did it go?"

"I'm fine. I've found the culprit. I double-checked to make sure." I handed him the camera. "Where's Angelica?"

"I'm here, dear. She entered the room, dressed casually in blue jeans, a sky-blue shirt, and white sneakers. I did a double take. It was super rare to see her out of uniform. "How did your fact-finding mission go?"

Will looked up from the camera. "Very well… or not, depending how you look at it."

She held out her hand, and he gave her the camera. Her poker face slid into place before she scrolled through the photos. She finished and magicked the camera away—it was in her hand, then it wasn't. Will grabbed my hand and led me to the Chesterfields. "Why don't we have a seat and discuss this… latest development." We sat next to each other, and Angelica sat opposite.

"Well," Angelica started, "that was unexpected." That about summed it up. There wasn't much else to say, really.

Will gave her a sympathetic look. "The question is, why? And how is he connected to that other fellow."

"I take it you haven't figured out who he is."

"Not yet, dear. But we're working on it. I called the news station and spoke to that reporter, but she didn't have any information on him. He only gave her a first name, and we can assume it's fake. His magic signature isn't in the system. We'll have to use our ingenuity to figure this out."

Hmm. "Could you interrogate Dr Finnegan? He must know who he is."

Will cocked his head to the side. "Not necessarily. Maybe the ringleader is making his demands or requests anonymously. Or maybe he's doing things through a third party."

"And no matter what, dear, we can't interrogate Dr Finnegan yet. Secrecy is a better weapon for now. We don't want our quarry knowing we're coming for them. Whoever's behind it has one huge fault: arrogance. It will be the reason we catch him. We have to plan this carefully. I'm going to sleep on it, and I suggest you both do the same. We'll reconvene tomorrow, discuss it, then set things in motion. His behaviour's escalating—James sent me a message late last night. The message for Chad was that a disaster the likes of which the PIB has never seen before is going to happen in the next few days. He's dared them to stop him. I intend to do just that." She raised her chin and looked every inch our leader. Pride and relief warmed my chest. If anyone could make this happen, it was Angelica.

"Do you have any idea what he plans to do?" I asked.

"He supposedly left a clue in what he said to Chad. Chad didn't have the wherewithal to take a photo of it, so let's hope what he repeated to James was accurate. James sent me this message." She magicked her phone to her hand and brought up the message, then leaned across the low table between the Chesterfields and handed me the phone. I angled it so Will could read at the same time.

What a shame—the Fair Lady must watch helplessly from afar as it all comes tumbling down. So, I have a new agent to play with. Welcome to my game, Chad. Things have never been more serious. What am I going to do next? Better look out—we're unbeaten, power-ful. We're coming for what's ours. Soon.

My heart beat double time as I read. "Are you the Fair Lady?"

Angelica leaned back. "On the face of it, I would say yes —I certainly feel helpless enough, and, right now, I am watching the PIB tumbling down. Depending on what happens next, it could be the end of us."

My eyes opened wide. I never would have thought she'd reached that level of despair and admission—you would never know to look at her. My gaze was fierce as I tried to put all my support and belief in her into it. "You're not and never will be. I know you'll overcome this, and we're all behind you, or next to you… whatever you need. If you can't solve this, no one can."

She gave me a small smile. "Thank you, dear. That means a lot."

I looked at the screen again and read the message a few more times. "Any other ideas? Do you think there are any clues in it?"

Will rubbed his nose. "Maybe. My instincts tell me there are—he's playing a game. He's said it more than once. It's not much of a game if he's running around creating havoc, and we're chasing him after the fact. Unless it's just about him scoring points. But where's the fun in playing a game with someone so much worse than you? I remember playing rugby at school. Our team was one of the best in all the county schools. It was never much fun when we beat a team sixty to nil. If you can win with your eyes closed, there's no testing of skills, pushing yourself, achieving your best. Unless this guy just likes to watch the PIB flounder, and he enjoys our added confusion?"

Angelica fiddled with the top button on her shirt. "He told us what he was doing last time. He enjoyed watching us scramble and still be unable to stop it. It wouldn't surprise me if he's giving us clues, and us missing them is his way of saying he's better than us again."

I handed Will the phone. Leaning forward, I put my elbows on my thighs and rested my face in my palms. "What's he got planned? Any ideas? I mean, he's cursed PIB agents, stolen money from one of the biggest banking institutions in the UK, killed five innocent people with lightning strikes… now what? I hate to think of the magnitude of it if it's going to be the worst one yet." Nausea twisted in my belly and thickened in my throat.

A knock sounded on the reception-room door. I looked at Angelica. "Are you expecting anyone?"

"Yes. Imani. Can you let her in, dear?"

I jumped up and hurried to answer the door. The little video monitor outside the room—a new addition—showed Imani patiently waiting. I opened the door and smiled. "Hey, stranger! Haven't seen you for a few days."

"Here I am, love, in all my reinstated magical glory." She grinned and flung her arms in the air.

I laughed and locked the door. "Come on through, Miss Fabulous."

"Don't you know it." She emphasised her hip sway as she strutted to the living room. Imani sat next to Angelica, and Will handed her the phone so she could read the message. After a minute, she gave the phone back. "Hmm. There's definitely something in that, but what? Have any of you come up with anything?"

"We think Angelica is the fair lady, for obvious reasons, and the PIB is going to come tumbling down—like that old nursery rhyme about London Bridge." Even though I'd grown up in Australia, having the British roots we did, every kid knew that one. The song played in my head. At least the tune wasn't too bad, but I still didn't want it on loop in my head for the whole day.

Will and Angelica looked at each other. He said, "You don't think… do you?"

She nodded slowly. "It's possible. But what?"

It took me a moment before I got what they were on about. "You think he'll attack London Bridge?" They both nodded. "So what do we do? Camp out there for a few days? At least we know what he looks like, so when he turns up, we can nab him."

Angelica leaned back and crossed her legs. "We could. But what if we're wrong and we miss the opportunity to stop what he's really going to do?"

Imani spoke. "I'm all for doing something. Maybe send Will and me to watch the bridge while you, James, and Lily keep pondering the message. Let us know if you come up with anything else."

The longer they talked about it, the more unsettled I became. "Would his clue really be that easy? Or what if it's a trick to get agents there just so he can hurt them or strike somewhere where they're not?"

"We can't know for sure, dear. All we can do is prepare for any eventuality. At least there's one thing he doesn't know, and that's that we have our powers back. He probably isn't expecting much PIB presence anywhere, to be honest. More than two thirds of our force have been affected by the curse. Even though they struck when there weren't many agents at headquarters, the alarm drew everyone afterwards, which is exactly what they wanted." She looked between Will and Imani as she spoke. "Because no one knows you can both travel, you should be able to come and go without notice, but leave your phones at home, just in case one of the directors has managed to bug them. Where's yours, Imani?"

She grinned. "At home. I figured as much."

"Good work. Make sure you keep out of sight. Find somewhere inconspicuous." Will angled his head down and gave her a look that said, "How long have I been doing this for?" Angelica kept her boss face on, giving no apologies whatsoever. Such an Angelica thing to do. "And you both know what he looks like." Will and Imani nodded. "In the meantime, Lily and I will do our best to track down who he is."

Will stood. "Sounds like a plan. I'll grab a burner phone while we're out so we can keep you updated." He placed his phone on the table. "Don't worry about answering it if it rings. Let it go to messages."

Imani stood and looked at Will. "Where to?"

"Tower Bridge. We can travel to the landing spot at Tower Hill tube station. That bridge is the perfect spot to watch from—crowded and far away enough that he'll never notice us watching, yet it has an unimpeded view. I'll also take these." He held his hand up, and a pair of large binoculars appeared. "PIB issue." He smiled as if that explained everything. It kind of did, but not totally.

"What's so great about PIB ones?" If I didn't ask, no one would volunteer the information.

Will answered, "They're made using magic, so you don't have to perform a spell when you use them. They can focus much further than normal ones of this size, and their field of vision is wider. And if I want to use my magic to send it an image of what the quarry looks like, it will highlight him by putting a little red arrow over his head, pointing at him.

All images are recorded as well, kind of like a video camera. I guess it's a video camera with a super-duper zoom lens."

Imani magicked her coat on. "We'll wear no-notice spells so we don't get asked to move on for being suspicious. This will be a cinch." Another pair of those special binoculars appeared in her hand.

Will magicked his gun to himself, pocketed it, and moved to the middle of the room where there was some space. "See you ladies later. I'll text you my number as soon as I grab a phone. Keep me updated, and I'll do the same." He made the doorway.

"Bye," Imani said, then stepped through. Will followed on her heels, and they disappeared.

A chill rippled through me. Guns meant potentially deadly stuff, and only specially trained police here carried them. Most police didn't have one. The PIB was a special case, and when dealing with dangerous witches, you needed every self-defence mechanism you could get.

"Right!" Angelica said rather loudly.

I jumped in fright. "Oh my God. Did you have to do that?" I slowed my rapid breathing.

"Sorry, dear. I'm just keen to start. Here." Her magic skimmed my scalp, and a thick, A4 blue display folder appeared on the table. "Have a look through that. Read everything and tell me your thoughts."

I picked it up. "What's in here?"

"Lots of plastic sheets filled with information on the prisoners who were killed in the blast the other day. James sent it to me this morning. I haven't had a chance to look through it yet. I was hoping you could do that while I *examine* Dr Finnegan more closely." She waggled her eyebrows, obviously referencing her terrible pun. It was nice to not be the only person who had questionable humour. I chuckled. "We did background checks when he first joined, but that was fourteen years ago. I'll start on the laptop, but I'm going to need to go out later."

I stood. "Okay. Let's do this. I'm going to set myself up on the kitchen table—it'll be easier to spread out. But make sure you tell me when you're going out. Maybe take my phone and leave yours here—no one is tracking me at the moment, as far as I know."

"Good idea."

I shuffled off to the kitchen and magicked myself a cup of coffee—most things were better while drinking it. I was sure the only good thing about most meetings was the catering. At least it gave people something to look forward to. Shame all meetings weren't catered.

It took me some time, but I eventually had a pile of paper representing the deceased criminals. Their crimes ranged from embezzlement to murder, and their sentences varied. Overall, twenty-six inmates had been killed—a sizable number—and two prison guards. Once I'd established who'd been killed and who'd survived, I read each file, starting with the dead criminals. All up, there were three hundred and seventy prisoners in the witch lock-up. And every inmate who died was a member of the same gang. They called themselves the Shadow Banes. Looked like they weren't as lethal as they thought.

It had taken three hours, but I was done. I took my notes to Angelica, who was on her laptop in the living room. She looked up and around as she was facing the window. "Have you got something for me?"

"I sure do." I handed her the book and sat on the other Chesterfield. "Every inmate killed was in the same gang. They managed to wipe out the entire group. Looks like this could have originated from inside the prison, unless everyone in that gang was just unlucky to be in that section at the time, but it seems unlikely. They were even less lucky than the guy who's been hit by lightning three times." Although, maybe that guy was lucky since he'd survived all three strikes.

She stared at me, her face aghast. "Are you sure one man has been hit three times?"

"Yep. I saw it on Facebook."

She smirked. "Oh, it must be true then."

"It was just shared there. I think it was originally a news thing. Whatever." For once, I didn't care if she made fun of me—we needed to get to the reason the gang had been wiped out. Was it accidental or deliberate? "Do you think it was an inside job?"

"Hang on a minute, dear, and let me read your notes." She took her time going through them and magicked some of the papers from the dining table to herself. She looked through everything. "Hmm, you're right."

I refrained from saying, "Der, I know," but I couldn't resist rolling my eyes. Why did she always have to question my work? I was awesome, dammit! "What do you think?"

"I think I'd like to look at the rest of the files. I only have the files for the deceased." She stood and made her way out of the room. I followed her to the kitchen, where she poured over the printouts on the table. She picked out one piece of paper and studied it. When she looked at me, excitement shone in her eyes. "I knew there was something familiar about our lightning guy." She handed me the paper.

I sucked in a breath. "Wow, they sure resemble each other. This could be his brother." The man on the page had similar facial features and looked to be in his early twenties. The biggest difference was the tattoo covering his neck and jawline. It wasn't clear what it was, but there was lots of green, black, and red.

"I'm betting it is. Byron Lord. Convicted for making and selling drugs and three counts of attempted murder for blowing up a rival gang member's drug lab. He's serving the second year of a twenty-five-year sentence. His father, also a career criminal, was killed four years ago by a PIB agent in self-defence. His brother's name is Shamus. Hang on a moment." Her laptop appeared on the table. She sat in front of it and typed while I sat next to her and observed.

After a few minutes of hopping from one site to the next, she ended up on Facebook at Simone Lord's page. Her details page didn't have anything about linked family members, but there were public photos of her with her two sons and another man—whether he was her partner, brother, or simply a friend, it was impossible to tell. But there was no mistaking her two sons and the comments from friends, which included, *You and your boys are looking fab*!

"Do you think Shamus was responsible for the explosion? Maybe trying to break his brother out? Or did his brother put him up to it to kill his enemies?"

"That's something we need to find out. Plus, we must get physical proof of everything. This is all speculation, especially Dr Finnegan's role in it. We can't show anyone your photos, plus, they wouldn't mean anything to them in isolation—it's an innocent photo of the doctor; that's it. He could be our key to this."

"But we have the magical signature used at the thefts plus at the PIB. That will tie Shamus to it."

"True, but if his brother is involved, we want to make sure he's punished too. Give him longer in jail. I don't want to spook anyone. Once they know we're after them, it will make it so much harder. I don't trust the new guy to get the job done without bungling it. And if Dr Finnegan knows we're onto him, he'll run."

"So why is Shamus taunting us? Surely he'd want to move as stealthily as possible?"

She shrugged. "Why does anyone do what they do? He might have an ego problem, or he hates us. We did imprison his brother and kill his father. In fact, I was on the team investigating organised crime when his father was killed, and I led the team that put his brother away. He has every reason to despise me."

"Well, what do we do now?" A loud knock came from the reception room. "I'll get it." I stood and hurried over. The screen showed James waiting within. I opened the door. "Hey, what are you doing here?"

"We got another message. Whatever is happening at the bridge is happening soon. The message said he was bored and felt like implementing his next plan by midnight. I didn't tell Chad what we thought—I don't want him spooking the guy or mucking anything up."

"Right, well, we have some news too. Maybe go into the kitchen and see Angelica." I would have loved to have told him, but she was really running the show, and she would know exactly what to tell James; then they could decide what to do next. During my organisation of the criminal files, Will had texted me his new number, so I guessed we'd be contacting him with all the details as soon as James and Angelica had finished their chat.

We joined Angelica in the kitchen and sat at the table. He gave her the latest news, and she reciprocated. She looked at her watch. "It's two thirty. We potentially have nine and a half hours. Let's hope he doesn't act earlier."

"Are you going to try and catch him before he gets there? James would be able to get his address."

James bit his bottom lip. "We'll suss it out, but unless I notify headquarters, I won't be able to get a warrant, and I don't know that it's wise to tell them. They'll likely stuff it up, and once he knows we're coming, he'll go to ground, and then who knows what havoc he'll cause. If we go without their knowledge and something goes wrong, it will be exactly what the directors need to get rid of Ma'am for good, and they might even lay charges."

"Crap."

Angelica nodded. "Crap, indeed." She took a deep

breath. "Let's not focus on what we can't do. We must concentrate on what we can do." She turned to my brother. "I'd like you to take this information"—she waved at the paperwork lying on the table—"and say Olivia helped you sift through it. Get permission to interview the inmates—specifically Byron. Obviously, interview the other ones in his gang too, concentrate on the weaker ones, those lower down the food chain. They may know less, but they're more likely to cave and give you information. Anything about the motivation for the jail catastrophe would be helpful."

I knew it was wrong, but I had to suggest it. "Can't he subtly compel Byron to talk?"

Angelica's disappointment was palpable. "Prisoners have rights, too, and if James was to get caught, he would face jail time. I'm not going to risk it—we have enough problems. And I can't see Chad approving something like that either. He might be stupid, but he's a rule follower—that's why they've put him there. They know he'll be motivated to 'do the right thing' by the bureau, in other words, find dirt on the misbehaving Agent DuPree." She rolled her eyes. "We have to play this by the book as much as possible."

"I'm sure I can get Chad to agree once he sees this. He may be stupid, but he does have the bureau's best interests at heart—at least his perception of what they are. I'll let you know how I go. And if you need backup in London, ping me."

Angelica gave a nod. "Will do."

James focussed on me. "If you go with them, be careful, do what you're told, etcetera, etcetera. Okay?"

"Yeah, yeah, I'll be careful and obedient." I held my hands up as if they were paws, stuck my tongue out, and panted like a dog.

He rolled his eyes. "You're insufferable. You know that?"

I grinned. "I like to think of it as I give as good as I get."

He stood and magicked all the pages into the folder and then the folder into his hand. "Well, just come back safely. I take it you'll travel the suspect straight to the PIB?"

"Yes," said Angelica. "I'm willing to take full responsibility. It shouldn't get me into too much trouble because we have his magic signature on file. But if we do arrest him, we'll have to figure out how to deal with Dr Finnegan ASAP. We don't have any evidence—other than Lily's photographs—linking him to Shamus, and I don't like our chances of getting Shamus to talk. But it is what it is because we're running out of time." She looked at her watch again. "That's another fifteen minutes gone." Uneasiness slithered through me, and the hairs on my arms jumped to attention. What was he going to do, and could we stop it in time?

"Right. I'll see you both later." James made his doorway and left.

I wasn't convinced we were doing the right thing. Niggling acid churned in my stomach. "We're missing something. I have a feeling, but I can't figure it out."

"I'm afraid that whether we are or not, we've reached a point where we have to act on the information we have. Taking everything into account, we're doing the best we can, and I think we've made the right decisions." She had years of experience, and countless successful operations to her name. I just had to trust she was right.

I swallowed the rising vapour of fear. "When do you want to go?"

"There's no better time than the present."

I could beg to differ, but since when did that get me anywhere? When she stood and made her doorway, I magicked my coat on and did the same, but an unwelcome thought bombarded my brain.

We were missing something, and it was critical.

If only I knew what it was….

CHAPTER 13

Angelica set a brisk pace, and the walk from the crowded tube station to Tower Bridge only took five minutes. On the way, we donned our no-notice spells. Sombre clouds loomed overhead, casting the river in an eerie half-light. Would that make it harder for Will and Imani to make out Shamus, even with their whizz-bang binoculars?

We found Will first, on the footpath just before the first tower. He was standing tall, a menacing yet sexy man in his black coat, looking through binoculars towards London Bridge, half a mile to the south.

"Any luck?" Angelica asked.

He lowered the binoculars and turned to her. "Nothing." Despite the long day of looking at pretty much nothing, his grey eyes were bright, alert. Nothing was going to get past him. "What about you? Find anything?"

She made a bubble of silence. "Our little friend is called Shamus Lord. James is going to get permission to interview Shamus's brother, Byron, in jail."

Will's forehead wrinkled. "That name rings a bell."

"That's because you were part of Strike Force Penguin."

"Ah, I remember that. Byron's a bloody nasty character."

"That he is," she said. "He's managed to wipe out a rival gang. We think that's what the explosion at the prison was all about."

He looked over Angelica's shoulder into the distance for a moment, likely thinking. Then he jerked his head towards London Bridge. "And what's all this about?"

Angelica's voice was matter of fact. "I'm betting on revenge. Just like the deaths at the prison."

"But why now? Why do both?" Will asked.

My hackles rose. Of course the two must be linked. Maybe that had been obvious to everyone else, but realisation took a while to dawn with me. Sometimes I was as bright as an Icelandic winter. As I pondered the question, Angelica said something to Will about going to speak to Imani, who was, apparently, at the other end of the bridge. I leaned against the railing and looked out over the muddy Thames towards London Bridge.

What were we missing?

Will stood next to me and raised his binoculars to watch the bridge. "What's up? You're unusually quiet."

"I know you guys are the best at what you do, but I can't shake the feeling that we've missed something… something crucial." My memory wasn't the best part of my brain, so I had to ask, "Do you remember exactly what the message was?"

"It was, 'the Fair Lady must watch helplessly from afar as it all comes tumbling down. So, I have a new agent to play with. Welcome to my game, Chad. Things have never been more serious. What am I going to do next? Better look out—we're unbeaten, powerful. We're coming for what's ours. Soon.'"

"I guess that bit about having a new agent to play with isn't important. I can't see what it would mean other than what it says. The Fair Lady must watch helplessly from afar." The nursery rhyme played through my head. I wasn't game to sing it because I wasn't known for my sweet voice. *London Bridge is falling down, falling down, falling down, London Bridge is falling down, my fair lady*. But if she was the woman on London Bridge, she wouldn't be watching it fall from afar. "Will?"

"Yes."

"Some people think Tower Bridge is London Bridge, don't they?"

"Yes."

My heart raced as I considered the next question. "What if they're actually going to make something happen to this bridge?"

He lowered his binoculars and stared at me. His brow furrowed. "I don't know. I don't know which one it is. You're right, though—it could be either one."

The message still trampled through my brain. *What am I*

going to do next? Better look out—we're unbeaten, powerful. We're coming for what's ours. Soon. Was that question answered in what he said afterwards? *Better look out—we're unbeaten, powerful.* It's kind of threatening, but not really, more like bragging. Why would he state the obvious? It didn't seem like his thing. What was hiding in there?

"Can you open your burner phone?"

"Why?"

"I want to type those words in and see what they look like."

He scrunched his face but unlocked the phone and passed it to me. I pulled up the Notes app and typed it in. *Better look out—we're unbeaten, powerful.* After studying it for a couple of minutes my breath hitched. My heart raced. I jerked my head up, nausea rising in my throat. "Will, look." I handed him the phone. "Read what the first letters of every word spell." Now that I'd noticed, I couldn't unsee it. How had we missed this? "What am I going to do next?"

"Blow up." His eyes widened. "This isn't a coincidence. We have to get everyone off this bridge. Now!"

"How the hell are we going to do that? And what if I'm wrong? What if it's London Bridge, like we originally thought? We're going to cause panic. What if it's for nothing? How do we explain that? Angelica will get fired for sure, and probably you too."

"We have to get people off both bridges, no matter the cost. Now you've deciphered it, I can't believe we didn't figure it out. Let's get Angelica and Imani." He grabbed my hand and pulled me along. If I was right, and this was the bridge he was going to blow up, he'd probably seen Will and Imani, and now Angelica. He had no idea who I was, but it didn't matter—if we'd been spotted, maybe he was about to detonate everything earlier. Double, triple crap with a cherry on top.

As we ran, I swivelled my head this way and that, looking out for him. God, there were so many people crossing the bridge, as well as cars and buses. This could be a catastrophe. Because we had our no-notice spells activated, we almost crashed into a few people—no one was getting out of our way. As we dodged around and through, my breath came fast.

Angelica and Imani saw us when we were closing in. Imani's eyes were wide, but Angelica had her poker face on, ready to hear the news we were obviously so desperate to tell her. We came to a puffing halt, and Will let it all come out. "He's going to blow it up. And it could be this bridge or London Bridge. We can't be sure. We need to evacuate."

My gaze zigzagged frantically along the bridge and to the footpath. He'd be unlikely to actually be on the bridge when it blew up, unless he was into drama and intended to pop away at the last minute. The rest of the message whispered in my head, *We're coming for what's ours.* The prison? Was he going to break out his brother after this? Was *we* his gang?

I didn't want to heap more on Angelica's head, but James was at the prison. What if something happened to him? "He's going to break his brother out. They're after *what's theirs*. That has to be the link. We have to tell James."

Will pressed buttons on his phone and put it to his ear. I could have kissed him for taking me seriously. "Hey, mate. Be prepared. They're coming to break Byron out…. Yes, I'm sure. We can't. We have our hands full here. Gotta go. Bye." He slipped the phone back in his coat pocket. He fixed his intense stare on Angelica. "What do you want to do? It's your call."

While hundreds of lives were teetering on the narrow balance beam between life and death, Angelica had to decide. There was nothing I could do. Or was there?

I magicked my camera to myself and turned it on. "Show me where Shamus was one minute ago." I didn't know if my magic could be that accurate, but it was worth a shot. If this worked, we'd have the upper hand. If it didn't…

Pointing my camera towards the end of the bridge, nothing much had changed, but I was sure the person in the bright-green jumper hadn't been standing there a second ago. I looked over the top of the camera to make sure. Yep, we had gone back only slightly in time. Even so, it wasn't going to be easy to spot Shamus in the crowd. But I had to try.

I looked carefully at the still image, then panned up— what if he was watching from a window somewhere? We'd never find him. It couldn't be helped. *Just ignore that, Lily, and do what you can.* As I moved slowly in a circle, I hoped like hell I'd see him.

"Lily, what are you doing?" Will came and stood next to me.

I lowered the camera. "Looking for him." I checked, and the bubble of silence was still around us from before. I whispered, "It lets me go back one minute." I didn't want to elaborate. He should understand, unless he was a lot dumber than I'd given him credit for.

"That's fantastic. Let me know if you find him. In the meantime, brace yourself."

"Huh? Why?" I swivelled my head around quickly, expecting an attack.

"We've decided how to evacuate the bridge, but it's going to leave us tired and exposed. We'll need you to watch over us while we're doing it. But don't go anywhere. Finding Shamus is going to have to take second place to saving people. We can't wait for him to act and take us by surprise."

"What if you evacuate it and he stays and waits?"

"I guess that's where your skills come in. It will give us time to find him."

"But what if he leaves and comes back later, when everyone is on the bridge again? You won't be able to keep them off it forever."

He put his hands on his hips. "We don't have time for that now. We have to do the best we can right now, and that's saving as many people as possible. If he knows we're here, he'll move sooner rather than later. He won't want us to have the upper hand. Also, he can assume that once we get everyone off the bridge, we'll keep them off it as long as we have to. His chance will be lost."

"Will!" Angelica's voice was firm and insistent.

Time was up.

Imani and Angelica jogged towards the end of the bridge, where it met the land. Will and I followed. I created my return-to-sender spell and kept my senses open to other people's magic. There was no time to find him in the crowd. Maybe he wasn't even here. Fear shot an arrow of adrenaline through me nevertheless, and my heart raced. Not knowing was torture, and as someone who hated surprises, it couldn't be worse.

When we reached the end of the bridge, Angelica and Imani stopped and turned. They joined hands with Will, making a circle. Angelica looked at me. "We'll have to drop our other spells when we do this, dear. Can you please protect us with a return to sender and a no notice?"

I nodded vigorously. "Of course. Do you want them now?"

"Yes please."

I concentrated on making the spells cover each person, one at a time, but because their hands were linked, the spells seemed to seep from one to the next. I instinctively knew that if they dropped hands, they'd all be vulnerable again. It was almost as if my magic *told* me. Not that there were voices in my head… at least, not yet. Anyway, there was nothing to be done for it. I'd have to be ready to cast individual spells if they split up.

Angelica's magic hummed along my scalp first, Imani's and Will's following quickly. The sensation started softly but gradually became more stifling, until the three entities became one powerful mass controlled by Angelica. Because I was using my magic, my other sight had kicked in unasked, and the trio were outlined by blue light, the brightest of which enveloped Angelica. Thank goodness the crowd of sightseers and Londoners going about their business couldn't see what I could. Although, that might be one way to clear the bridge....

Not wanting to have my back to a possible attack, I forced myself to turn around and observe my surroundings. Still no sign of Shamus. I took a deep breath against the onslaught of powerful vibrations. Then vibrations of another sort began.

The ground rumbled. My heartrate spiked, but then I realised no new magic had come into play. This must be how they were going to clear the bridge. The rumbling grew louder, and the ground shook. A man cried, "Earthquake!"

The bridge shuddered. People ran. Screams echoed from everywhere. Mothers picked children up and ran off the bridge. Men in suits, older people, everyone scattered and moved as fast as they could. An old lady tripped and fell. I was about to run over and help her when another woman intervened and helped her up and past me. And still, the bridge shook.

Despite the cold, sweat beaded on Angelica's forehead as she stared at the bridge. A handful of people were still on it

—evacuating from the upper levels was going to take way longer than the lower ones.

And then new magic bombarded my scalp, pressing on it painfully. The manic energy was one I recognised from the day of the curse. It came from the other side of the bridge. I had to assume it was Shamus. We couldn't let him blow up the bridge, for God's sake! People were still on it, and it was Tower Bridge, a national treasure.

There was only one answer. I had to get to Shamus, and quickly. It might have been the dumbest thing I'd ever done, but I had to try. I knew Angelica, Will, and Imani were okay —they weren't in his line of fire. It was time to go.

I ran.

"Lily, no!" cried Will.

I ignored him, focussing on getting to the other side as quickly as possible. I also kept my other sight trained on my surroundings as I sprinted—if any spell descended, I'd have a second to see it before it went off. Maybe there was a chance I could counteract it.

The shaking halted. My friends must have stopped the earthquake now that most people were off or trying to get to land. They would have felt the other magic too. I dropped the spells protecting them because I'd need everything I had when I found Shamus.

The frigid air scoured my throat as I sucked in breaths and forced my arms and legs to keep up the pace. I desperately looked ahead, trying to spot Shamus, but the crowd watching the bridge from the shore was so thick, it was impossible to find him.

I'd only reached the middle of the bridge. Damn.

His magic built. Whatever he was doing, it was happening now.

I stopped running and looked back. Imani, Will, and Angelica were catching up. We were the only ones on this level of the bridge, but people were pouring out of the tower ahead, having come down from the upper level.

I didn't think it was possible, but I had to try. I planted my feet. Throwing my arms wide, I opened my portal and waited.

Imani and Ma'am ran past me, towards the other side of the bridge, but Will stopped. "Don't do this, Lily. It's too dangerous."

I spared him a quick glance. "I have to try. And there's no time to argue, so please don't distract me."

He heavy sighed. "You're going to be the death of me." He shook his head as if he couldn't believe what he was about to say. "Keep doing what you're doing. I'll protect you this time." I gratefully dropped my return to sender as his spell enveloped me. I needed every drop of energy I could get.

I reached my magical senses out. Shamus's energy was building, gathering, pushing up from underneath, but until I knew what the spell was, it would be hard to counteract it. Unless…. What I proposed had to be timed to perfection. If I moved too early, he'd stop what he was doing. If I reacted too late, there would be bits of Will and me exploding into the Thames. Something to be avoided if at all possible, and

I wasn't ready to die. Not today. Not for many years to come.

I drew magic into every vein, pore, and cell, sucked it in until I was feverish and ready to spontaneously combust. I shut my eyes and listened, felt for his magic, for the moment his spell came into being. If I caught it at the right moment, he would be too taxed to do it again, and by then, Angelica and Imani would hopefully have found him.

I breathed in through my nose, the air thick and briny. The screaming had stopped. Sweat trickled down the sides of my face. I so wanted to rip my coat off, but this wasn't the time. My stomach expanded as the magic fought to get out, but I held it in. I gritted my teeth and slowed the flow of power but allowed a tiny bit more in. I was at my maximum. How much longer could I hold it?

An electrical pulse zapped the back of my neck.

My eyes shot open, and I said, "Encapsulate."

The scalding magma of power burst through me as Shamus's spell expanded and ignited. The bridge buckled upwards, expanding with the pre-blast force. I sucked in more power and imagined it flowing over the explosion, encapsulating it.

This was going to hurt.

His magic was about to burst through. He must have felt my magic near his, and he shot more power into it. Searing agony engulfed my stomach as I called on even more power. I was losing control. His explosion was close to breaking free.

No! I wouldn't let it happen.

I braced myself and drew more and more. The cacophony of turbulent rushing water filled my ears—the magical river racing and churning. I screamed and threw it all against the blast, a rush of magic sizzling from my fingertips. Tears from the pain streamed down my face.

"Lily!"

One last blow against my shield. I fell to my knees and gave everything I had to push back. His spell faltered, my magic absorbing the impact. I grunted as the fury of it crashed into my stomach and chest, flinging me upwards and off my feet, but before I could be thrown back, strong hands grabbed me and pulled me down.

Shamus's magic fizzled out. My knees gave way, but those strong hands held me tight, didn't let me fall. I forced my legs to hold my weight as I reached my awareness out for any signs of Shamus's power. Electricity sparked in the air, an echo of our battle, but that was all.

I slowed my breathing. Dizziness engulfed my head. I swayed but stayed upright. If Shamus had anything left and tried again, I would fail. I was spent.

I opened my eyes. Will's fierce gaze drilled into mine, seeking reassurance that I was okay. Other than the need to cry, I was pretty sure I'd live. "I'm fine, but I have nothing left."

The tension around his eyes stayed, but his lips quirked up into a crooked smile. "You don't say? Surprising since you hardly raised a sweat." My pathetically weak fist bumped his arm. He laughed and pulled me in for a squishy hug, which didn't last long enough. "We need to check on

Angelica and Imani. I could feel lots of magic before, but there's nothing now. I hope they caught him." Unlike me, Will couldn't tell people's magics apart. "Are you okay to walk?"

"Should be. Maybe go on ahead. I'll catch up."

His brow furrowed. "No can do. I'm drained but not as bad as you. I'm strong enough to defend you if I have to. If anything happened to you, I'd never forgive myself."

I took a deep breath and shoved out the voice telling me I wanted to sit down… or was that lie down and go to sleep? "Let's go."

Will slipped his gun out as we walked. I was all for the extra precaution. Even though I would likely be able to draw next to no magic, I stayed alert and kept the portal open, just in case.

Despite everything that had happened, I still had my no-notice spell up, and a quick look at Will's aura confirmed his was too. As we approached the milling crowd and the few police who appeared to be trying to calm everyone and find out exactly what had happened, no one gave us a first glance, let alone a second.

My eyes widened. Just to the left of the masses stood Angelica and Imani. They each held an upper arm of the man kneeling between them whose head was bent, wrists behind his back, likely restrained with Imani's PIB-issue, magic-stifling cuffs. The prisoner lifted his head as we approached, and he stared into my eyes.

His tone was scarred with hate. "You…" His flinty stare made my skin crawl. But I had nothing to fear. I'd beaten him, and with no access to his magic, he was harmless. With no energy to tell him what I thought of him, I shrugged. There was a reason "if looks could kill" was a cliché—it happened way too often.

"Bad luck, Donald Duck." I grinned, thinking of the quackmobile. Seems I had more energy left than I'd thought. As Shamus tried to laser me with his eyes, I turned my gaze longingly to the ground next to the tower. That looked like such a lovely place to sit and rest. I was about to turn, when my senses went on high alert. I followed Angelica's gaze to the path leading to the bridge.

He was back—the director who'd visited the prison disaster to tell Angelica she was on suspension, and he still had his stupid top hat on. How had he found us when no one had their phones on them? I narrowed my eyes. An enemy of Angelica's was an enemy of mine. Will looked at me and whispered, "Try and be more subtle. One day it might help to take him by surprise." Meh, what did I care? I was never going to be an agent. The only reason I toned it down was so I didn't get Will and Imani into more trouble than they might be in right now.

The growl low in my throat was involuntary. But there was good reason. Chad strode behind the director. What the hell was he doing here? Come to steal Angelica's glory? And don't get me wrong; I didn't hate Chad. He was an unwitting pawn in the directors' game, and other than being dumber than the average agent, he hadn't been evil... so far.

They both must have had no-notice spells on because

the crowd ignored them. A tall man in a business suit was arguing with one of the police, who had cordoned off the bridge. "I'm sorry, sir, but we'll need engineers to clarify the safety after that tremor. Being an isolated incident, there could be a fault with the structure. Please use London Bridge." The policeman pointed south. The man pressed his lips together and balled his fists but ended up walking away. Others followed as word spread and other police arrived.

Top Hat Guy spoke. "I should've known that you'd be where an extremely high magic reading came from. You set off all our alarms, Agent DuPree. Interesting to see you have your magic back." He extended his heavy glare to Imani and Will. Looked like I was flying under his radar. The less he knew about me, the better. "And who have you got there?"

"Shamus Lord. He was plotting to blow up the bridge. He was also behind the messages sent to the PIB, the thefts, and lightning murders."

"I hope you can prove all that."

"Of course I can. Here's exhibit A." Angelica held up a ring I recognised—a thick gold band with square emerald stone, the one he'd been wearing when I'd seen him on TV. "This is one of the artefacts stolen from HQ the other day. He's changed its form from when Dana had it, but it's the ring that magnifies power. He was wearing it when he attacked the bridge." She raised a brow as if to say, gotcha! I blinked. Wow, I'd beaten a witch who was using a power-enhancing tool. Was I stronger than I thought?

Top Hat Guy cleared his throat and held out his hand.

"Please pass the suspect to Agent Williamson the Third. He and Imani can transport him to a cell at headquarters, and I'll take that ring." She handed it to him. He slipped it in his pocket. "You're coming with me." Where was he taking her?

Angelica waited for Chad to reach the prisoner. Head held high, she stepped out of the way. "May I ask where we're going?"

Top Hat Guy frowned. With paler than pale skin, sunken cheeks, and saggy jowls, he didn't look too well. "The board would like to meet with you. The location, of course, is top secret. I'll make the doorway, and you'll go first." Just when I thought I was done with fear for the day, it coiled in my belly. I wouldn't trust this guy as far as I could throw him without magic. But Angelica didn't so much as flinch.

"Shall we?" she asked, her strong voice calm and businesslike.

Top Hat Guy made his doorway. As Angelica stepped through, he turned to Chad. "Take them all back to HQ and gather them for a meeting. I'd like some answers. Agent Bianchi will join you shortly."

Chad quickly nodded. "Of course, Sir." He gave an awkward bow, which Top Hat Guy turned his back on before shooting Will an angry glare, stepping through his doorway, and disappearing. He hadn't even thanked Angelica, Imani, or Will for capturing the guy and retrieving an artefact. Oh, that's right, he wouldn't have been happy because it made Angelica look good.

One hand gripping Shamus's shoulder, Chad turned to

Imani. "We haven't met. I'm Agent Williamson the Third, but you can call me Sir. What's your name, Agent?"

"Agent Jawara, Sir."

"Right, Agent Jawara, can you please make the doorway to the reception room in the cell sector?"

"Yes, Sir."

He turned to Will. "And you two can just go to the regular reception room. I'll see you in the boardroom in fifteen minutes."

"Yes, Sir."

As soon as Chad left, I frowned. "I hope Angelica's okay. I don't trust Top Hat Guy. He's as slimy as an oily naked person."

"What?" Will's mouth was stuck between horror and laughter. "You need practice with those analogies. You sure come up with some weird ones."

"What's wrong with that? It's true, isn't it?"

He chuckled. "I suppose it is. And don't worry about Angelica—she can take care of herself."

"If they do anything to hurt her, they'll have all of us to deal with." I held my fists up in a fighting stance, not that I knew how to fight. It was the thought that counted, and my magic was more than up to the task.

"Okay, Rocky, let's get back to HQ."

I took one last look at Tower Bridge standing proud and pretty. Thank God we'd figured things out when we did, or London would have lost a landmark and hundreds of lives. I blew out a huge relieved breath before using the last of my strength to make my doorway. Unfortunately, there was a chance my relief was premature. Was everyone I loved about to get fired?

⁂

As Will and I walked the corridor to the conference room, I asked, "Can you make a bubble of silence?"

"Sure." His magic tickled my nape. "Shoot."

"What are we going to do about Finnegan? We have no proof other than my photos, which we can't use." We didn't even know how far his betrayal ran. Had he helped Shamus gain access to HQ so he could spell everyone with the curse?

"We'll have to wait until Shamus admits it. In the meantime, we'll keep a close eye on Finnegan. It sucks, but he's going to get away with it for now."

I sighed. My stomach grumbled, and not only from hunger. Anger over the unfairness of it all rankled. Will opened the conference-room door for me. I gritted my teeth as I entered, tension rippling through me. Game face activated.

Everyone sitting around the table turned when we came in. James and Millicent were on the opposite side, Beren and Olivia were on our side, and Agent Lyon was at the foot of the table. Imani and Chad weren't back yet. He'd obviously underestimated the time it took to register a criminal into the system.

I sat next to Olivia, and Will went around the table to sit next to Mill, opposite me. I looked at James and tried to glean whether he knew what was going on. Had anything happened at the jail? If it had, at least he was safe. My enquiring stare received a subtle shake of the head. Fine.

A thought shook its squirrel tail in my face, demanding attention. Had Dr Finnegan purposely kept us from finding a cure for the curse? That made total, depressing sense. Shame we couldn't prove it. At least he wasn't in the room. I'd find it hard to hold back showing how I felt. Could they trust him to do his job properly from now on?

The door opened. We all shot our gazes to it. Chad walked in, followed by Imani, and Angelica. Chad looked relaxed enough. Imani had her best poker face on, as did Angelica, but an undercurrent of anger pulsed beneath the surface. Her stiff shoulders and firmer-than-usual footfalls attested to it. I'd known her long enough to figure her tells. She made it hard to know what she was feeling, but it wasn't always impossible.

What bombshell was about to be dropped?

I gripped the arms of my chair.

Chad stopped at the head of the table, pulled his chair out, and gave a nod to Angelica to sit to his right. She sat slowly, deliberately. I wouldn't want to be Chad or Top Hat Guy when she finally got her revenge.

Imani magicked an extra chair and squeezed it between me and Agent Lyon. I looked at her and got the same subtle head shake James had bestowed on me. And they called themselves my friends. Phooey to that.

Chad smoothed his tie down and sat back in his chair, making it lean far enough that he could cross his feet and place them on the table. My mouth dropped open. No way!

James blinked, and Millicent nudged him with her elbow. Angelica closed her eyes and took a deep breath, then opened them again.

"So, gang," Chad started. *Gang?* This wasn't off to a great start. I resisted the urge to look under the table for Scooby Doo. "Today something wonderful happened. Angelica and her sidekicks solved a grave crime. Because of their wonderful work, Shamus Lord is languishing in jail as we speak." I would hardly have called it languishing. He'd been in there for approximately ten minutes. Angelica's eye-roll spoke for all of us, but she had her face turned away from Chad, so he didn't see. Maybe a tad immature, but the alternative would be for her to laugh in his face, and that was even worse. Venting was probably way safer than Volcano Angelica erupting.

Chad's smile was self-satisfied—as if he'd had something to do with the outcome—and proud, as if Angelica was his loyal and competent subject. This meeting had so much potential to go pear-shaped. Would anyone mind if I magicked some popcorn in?

"Because Angelica has redeemed herself, the powers that be have agreed to reinstate her."

"Yay!" Everyone stared at me. Oops, had I said that out loud? I bit my top lip to stop anymore joy coming out. Funnily enough, Angelica and Imani didn't share in the joy. They both held firm to their poker faces. What had I missed?

"As I was saying, Angelica has been reinstated as my second in command. She's still on probation, but I would like you to welcome her back to the fold." He clapped. It echoed around the shocked room. "Well, come on, folks, a bit of encouragement. It's been a tough week for Angelica, and she needs our support." Will and I exchanged incredulous glances.

Angelica grimaced, all poker-faced restraint gone. Her chest rose as she took a deep breath. "Thank you, Agent Williamson the Third. I would add to that, but I'm afraid I have nothing constructive to say."

He smiled kindly. "Don't worry about it. We all get tongue-tied sometimes. I'm sure it's just all the excitement of being back at HQ, hey?" He slapped her on the back. I sucked in a breath and held it.

The alarm blared. My heart stuttered and raced. I braced for that feeling of nausea. It didn't come. Chad's shocked arms flung in the air, and he pushed off the table with his feet. His chair shot backwards and tipped, spilling him onto the floor. Whatever. He could look after himself. He was a grown man after all.

Ma'am jumped to her feet, and James ran around the table, making it to the door first. He flung it open and ran through. Ma'am called to Millicent and Agent Lyon. "Secure the facility. No one goes in or out." Their magic zinged into life, probably creating a spell that would make it impossible for anyone to travel out with magic or otherwise. From what I knew of that protocol, all doors to the outside would automatically lock, and the lift would stop.

More magic bombarded me. It was familiar, and I should have expected it.

Dr Finnegan.

I grabbed Will's arm. "Dr Finnegan's magic. He's doing a spell. We have to get to his rooms now!"

He ran for the door and called out, "B, hurry!" Good thinking. Will and I were depleted. There was no way we'd take him on and win. At least he couldn't escape. I sprinted out the door, Beren close behind. Our feet slapped against the hard floor, but the blaring alarm drowned it out.

Will reached the infirmary first. He quickly looked back to check we were there, and, as he turned to enter, pulled his gun out. When we reached the doors, I moved aside to let Beren enter first. His magic would be needed, and there wasn't much I could do to help. The last thing I wanted was to be a liability and get in the way. Fully intending to stay out of it, I cautiously went in after Beren.

When I stepped into the empty room, the alarm died. I halted and tried to breathe quietly, which was difficult after running.

Voices came from the next room. I crept to the door, not wanting to be seen. It took me back to being ten and secretly listening into my parents' private conversation about what they were getting James and me for Christmas. Unfortunately, there was no happy ending to this eavesdropping expedition.

"Oh, nothing. Just tidying up after a busy day. Glad to see you're both better. How did you get rid of the curse? Is that what you came to talk about?" Dr Finnegan's voice was artificially happy, as if he were doing a commercial trying to convince the audience that the bathroom shower cleaner he held was the product to end all products. Just waving the bottle in the vicinity of the shower banished all mould. Yeah, right.

"It was by sheer luck I cured it, actually." Beren had his usual, easy-going voice happening. I supposed if you were going to go undercover, you needed top-notch acting skills.

"Excellent! Well, I actually have an appointment to get to. Do you think we could meet tomorrow to go over how you did it?"

"I hope the appointment is in the building." Will. "We're in lockdown. No one's going in or out for a while."

The conversation paused. "Oh, well. Um, do you know how long it will last? What happened?"

"Who can say?" Will was keeping his tone light. "We don't know yet. Agent Williamson the Third invoked lockdown protocol." He was keeping Ma'am's demotion and reinstatement a secret. She had taken control in that room, and everyone who was there knew it. Chad was a reasonable guy. Maybe he'd defer to her and be PIB leader in title only? One could hope. "Anyway, mind if we look around? Make sure everything's okay?" If that didn't clue Finnegan in, nothing would.

Goosebumps machine-gunned along my arms. I started to turn my head to look behind me, but a hand clamped over my mouth. I was slammed into someone's chest, and something sharp pricked the side of my throat. I'd unwittingly found our fugitive. Just my luck.

He breathed into my ear quietly, "Not so powerful now, are you? Told you all I was smarter, but you didn't listen.

And now you're going to help me free my brother from that hellhole jail you put him in. And in case you're wondering, that's a scalpel I have at your throat."

Oh, great. That was a piece of information I didn't need. I would have said something, but his hand was so tightly clamped over my mouth, it was impossible to speak. Firstly, I would never help him, even if I died for my choice, and secondly, I didn't have enough magic to help him tie his shoes. I was guessing he didn't either. He might have assumed I had more magic at my disposal since I beat him on the bridge. Nevertheless, he was the one with the knife at my throat.

The balance of power was his… for now.

"Make a noise, and I'll cut your throat." Well, der, thanks for stating the obvious. Shame I couldn't transmit my sarcasm by osmosis. "You're going to make a doorway to the jail." I carefully shook my head, hyperaware of the blade on my skin. He pressed it tighter. My throat stung as it pierced the skin.

I tried to mumble that I didn't know the coordinates, but his hand made it impossible to utter anything decipherable. Great. I was going to die because this idiot didn't know what I didn't know.

"What did I say about speaking? Now make that doorway. And don't try anything funny—I'll know if you do. My talent is reading spells as they're created. I just need you to make the doorway because I don't know the coordinates, and my magic signature is linked to your damn alarm."

I definitely didn't have power enough to make a doorway, but maybe I had enough in my personal stash to do something small yet effective. I was betting his claim was a load of poppycock. I had one chance to escape, and I was taking it.

As I fumbled inside for my own life source, I shut my eyes and concentrated on the metal tip at my neck. This was going to hurt, but I'd still be alive at the end of it if all went well. Surprise was going to be my friend for a change.

Breathing in the musky scent of his sweaty palm, I drew from deep inside and pushed the energy up to my throat and out into the scalpel. I leaned against Shamus when the dizzy spell hit, but I kept my life force flowing. *Make it red hot.*

It was done.

The sting of the blade intensified as it burnt my throat.

Shamus screamed and dropped the scalpel. "You evil bi—"

"Lily!" Will burst through the door. Not wanting to be a human shield, I grabbed the wrist of the hand at my mouth. I pulled his hand away just enough to change the angle. Then I fastened my teeth around his index finger and bit down hard. He screamed again and punched my back. I stumbled forward and smacked into Will. Casting a quick eye over me to make sure I was okay, our eyes met. Satisfied I was fine, he shoved me to the side, safely out of the way, then launched himself at Shamus.

Yelling came from the other room, and both Beren's and Dr Finnegan's magic prickled my scalp. A crash of something metallic hitting the floor came through the door, then a grunt, and swearing. Another smash and clatter, a thud.

I looked from the door to Will. Who should I help? Will had tackled Shamus, and they were wrestling on the ground. Surely Will had this covered—he was taller and bigger than his adversary, and he still had his gun. Decision made, I turned and ran into the next room.

Big mistake. Each man used his magic to throw things at the other as Beren chased Dr Finnegan around the room. I ducked just in time to avoid a metal bedpan flying at my head. It clanged into the wall next to the door.

Beren and the doctor dodged and weaved around a bed on wheels as implements, beakers, and cups sailed through the air. Every time one met its mark, someone grunted. A plastic chair sat forgotten next to the wall. A metal or timber chair would have been way better, but maybe this would be enough to distract Dr Finnegan long enough that Beren could take control. Goodness knew why he hadn't drawn his gun.

Both men must have known I was there, but they didn't dare take their eyes off each other. I had no magical protection, but hopefully Dr Finnegan wouldn't notice. If he did, I was in trouble. I grabbed the chair and moved closer to the melee.

Beren was at the head of the bed, and Dr Finnegan stood at the foot of it. All I had to do was stand as close to Dr Finnegan as possible and look menacing, and he'd have to pay attention, hopefully giving Beren a chance to achieve a winning blow.

Clang, smash. The crackle as someone trod on broken glass.

Moving slowly, I crossed the room, but when I was eight feet away, I leapt towards Dr Finnegan, chair raised. His head jerked around, and he aimed his hand at me, the words to a spell forming on his lips. Crap.

I brought my chair down towards his head. He shoved his arm up to protect himself as the last word of his spell left his mouth. An invisible wall of air careened into my stomach, sending me backwards through the air. My back slammed against the wall, and my head followed.

And that was the end of that.

⁂

Voices—male and female—mumbled. One voice in particular stood out. "Lily? Lily, wake up." I opened my eyes to a concerned Will. He was kneeling on the floor in front of me. I scrunched my eyes shut as a headache pierced the back of my head. "Lily!" He lightly slapped my face.

"Stop." I opened my eyes a crack. "I'm okay. I've got a major headache." I leaned forward and touched the back of my head. Sticky blood. Gah. "Did you get Shamus?"

"Yes. He's back in lock-up."

I was about to ask about Dr Finnegan when his protests stopped me. "Get these cuffs off me. I haven't done anything. I've been loyal to this organisation for more years than any of you. For God's sake, stop manhandling me."

Angelica must have run to get here so quickly. I would imagine not much time had passed from me hitting the wall and Beren getting the situation under control. "Why, Dr Finnegan? That's what I'd like to know."

He broke down and cried. Whoa, that was unexpected. Was he going to play the sympathy card? "You wouldn't understand. You don't have children."

She folded her arms. "Try me."

"Shamus is bad news. He's been dating my daughter, got her into drugs. She's even stolen from her mother and me. Our sweet little girl's turned into someone we barely recognise. She refused to give him up. As soon as we found out what's been going on with Dawn, I begged him to leave her alone. I even offered to pay him off, but he said he didn't want that. He said if I helped him free his brother, he'd leave Dawn alone, never speak to her again, disappear." He bowed his head.

Angelica looked at me, her eyes misty, but then she blinked, and it was as if the tears had never been there. "Oh, believe me, I understand. I'd do anything to protect the ones I love, but I'm afraid I can't help you. You've compromised the bureau, almost shut us down. You could've come to me. Maybe I could've helped you." She stepped close to him, but he didn't meet her eyes, keeping his gaze fixed on the floor. "I'm sorry, Paul, but you're under arrest." She turned to the two agents holding his handcuffed arms. "Take him to the cells."

Shoulders slumped, tears still falling, he let them take him away. I sucked in a deep, shuddering breath. Wow, that was awful. Beren knelt next to Will. "Here, Miss Fearless, let me take a look." He placed his hands on both sides of my head and probed around. After maybe a minute of warmth infusing my scalp, the headache faded away. "Done. I've healed your cut and the concussion. If you feel ill later, let me know, and I'll have another look. But you should be fine."

I gave him a tired smile. "Thanks, B. You're the best."

"Hey, I thought I was the best." Will raised a brow.

I grinned. "You are kind of cool, but the best? I would have said yes when you were the owner of a quackmobile, but as the owner of a regular car, not so much."

His mouth dropped open. When he recovered, he said, "Maybe I'll just have to prove it to you. Come on, and I'll take you home." He gave me a sexy smile.

He helped me stand. After saying goodbye to Beren and Ma'am, Will went to make his doorway when Chad strode casually into the room, his arms behind his back as if he had not a care in the world. "Ah, there you are, Agent DuPree."

Both Beren and Ma'am, answered, "Yes?"

Chad's forehead wrinkled as he looked from one to the other. "You're both DuPree?"

Ma'am heavy sighed. "Yes, Agent Williamson the Third; we're both DuPree. Which one of us do you want?"

"Well, you of course." He blushed. "Ah, Agent Pike was showing me how to use the handcuffs, and I got a bit stuck. He ran off before I could ask for help. To be honest, I thought I could work them out for myself." He brought both hands to the front and held out one arm. Yep, there was definitely a set of handcuffs hanging off it.

A set of keys popped into Ma'am's hand. "Here, Sir." She took his arm and freed him, then scooped the handcuffs up and shoved them in her belt. "Maybe leave the agenting to those of us who know what we're doing."

My eyes widened. Would she get away with that? He'd been pretty docile up until now, but surely that would offend him. He leaned closer to her and lowered his voice. "To be honest, I enjoy the organisation of things. I never could adjust to being in the field. I lasted three months early in my career. But this job is way more exciting than my position in New York. They'd shoved me in an office. I organised the roster, kept the weapons and ammunition stocked, that sort of thing. It was a big surprise when they moved me here. But I'm enjoying it."

"Well, why don't we come to an arrangement? You can oversee the day-to-day running of HQ administrations, and I'll deal with the cases and field operations."

"But I like sitting in on meetings. As long as I can still do that, you have a deal."

Ma'am held out her hand. "Deal. But it would behove both of us to not say anything to the directors."

"Of course." At least he seemed to understand something. Maybe having him here wasn't going to be as bad as we originally thought.

"Great." She turned her attention to Will and me. "Now everything's settled, it's time you two went home and had a well-deserved rest. I have everything under control." She gave us a satisfied smile.

We bade her goodbye, and as Will made his doorway, I

had no doubt she did have everything under control. Everything was as it should be. I looked down at my tattoo and frowned. Well, almost everything was as it should be. But there would be time enough to right that later. I'd make sure of it.

ABOUT THE AUTHOR

USA Today bestselling author, Dionne Lister is a Sydneysider with a degree in creative writing, two Siamese cats, and is a member of the Science Fiction and Fantasy Writers of America. Daydreaming has always been her passion, so writing was a natural progression from staring out the window in primary school, and being an author was a dream she held since childhood.

Unfortunately, writing was only a hobby while Dionne worked as a property valuer in Sydney, until her mid-thirties when she returned to study and completed her creative writing degree. Since then, she has indulged her passion for writing while raising two children with her husband. Her books have attracted praise from Apple Books and have reached #1 on Amazon and Apple Books charts worldwide, frequently occupying top 100 lists in fantasy and mystery.

She's excited to add cozy mystery to the list of genres she writes. Magic and danger are always a heady combination.